Aarya

Chasing Cosmic Chuckles

A Hare-Brained Hustle through
Time's Giggle Galaxy

Manisha Nagapudi

DEDICATION

To my family – my parents and sister, the original cast of the sitcom I never knew I needed—thanks for the endless episodes of drama, comedy, and occasional thriller.

To my friends, the irreplaceable gems in the tapestry of my existence. Your encouragement, all-day chats, and shared laughter have been the soundtrack of my life. This is for the bonds that time and distance cannot diminish, for the ones who have stood by me through thick and thin.

And to everyone who has wondered, questioned, or perhaps raised an eyebrow at my seemingly unconventional path—this is for you too. For the skeptics and the curious minds, I hope this work serves as a testament to the diverse paths we tread and the unique stories we each have to tell.

To all those who have shared in my victories, understood my struggles, and witnessed the evolution of my journey—thank you. Your presence, whether silent or vocal, has shaped the narrative of my life. This work is dedicated to the collective mosaic of individuals who have played a part in the tapestry of my existence.

May these words resonate with each of you, as a small token of gratitude for the threads you've woven into the fabric of my story.

CONTENTS

CONTENTS

Part 2

PROLOGUE

In the whimsical universe of Aarya's world, where social media dilemmas, awkward encounters, and unexpected revelations dance in the spotlight, a tale unfolds—a tale that transcends the ordinary and navigates the hilarious intricacies of modern life.

Meet Aarya, a protagonist caught in the comical web of societal expectations, nosy neighbours, and the perpetual chaos of her own decisions. As we embark on this journey, fasten your seatbelts for a rollercoaster ride through the corridors of Aarya's mind, where indecision wears the crown, and laughter echoes louder than the judgments of society.

This is not just a story; it's a satirical symphony, a humorous tapestry woven with the threads of social quirks, relationship shenanigans, and the perpetual quest for identity in a world that seems to be in a perpetual state of social media-induced frenzy.

As each chapter unfolds, get ready to laugh, cringe, and relate, for Aarya's tale is not just hers—it's a mirror reflecting the absurdities and joys of our own lives. So, turn the page and step into Aarya's world, where every misstep is a dance move, and every awkward encounter is a step closer to the grand finale of self-discovery. Welcome to the amusing chaos that is "Aarya"

Part 1

THE GREAT SOCIAL MEDIA DILEMMA

Once upon a time in the land of Likes and Retweets, there lived a young woman named Aarya. With a smartphone in one hand and a cup of coffee in the other, she found herself teetering on the precipice of a decision that would shake the very foundations of her virtual existence.

Aarya was a connoisseur of indecisiveness, a virtuoso of vacillation. Her inner compass wavered more than a politician in an election year, and today's quandary was no exception. The dilemma that plagued her: to deactivate or not to deactivate her social media accounts.

As Aarya scrolled through her various timelines, she couldn't escape the relentless bombardment of success stories, relationship updates, and the occasional cat video. Everyone seemed to be on a rollercoaster of life achievements, and Aarya felt like she was still waiting in line for her turn to board.

First in line was Rohan, her high school classmate, who just got a promotion at his job. He posted a picture of himself holding a plaque that read "Employee of the Month." Aarya couldn't help but wonder if he was the only employee.

Next up was Sara, her college roommate, who posted a picturesque photo of herself on a beach with a caption that read, "Living my best life!" Aarya, sitting in her Pjs on the couch, wondered if Sara's "best life" involved Photoshop or if she had just mastered the art of strategic cropping.

Then came the relationship statuses that read like the script of a romantic comedy. Couples getting engaged, married, or having babies—sometimes all in the same week. Shrithi, her distant cousin had just gotten engaged and put up a post that read:

🌸 ✦ Blessed to announce that after years of patient waiting, my heart has finally found its forever home! 💞 👫 ✦ The universe aligned, and the stars whispered tales of true love into my soul. 😍 📸 From the very first moment, it felt like destiny was orchestrating our love story. 💑 💕 To all those who said love takes time, thank you for your wisdom. It's true what they say—good things come to those who wait! 🙌 💖 Here's to a lifetime of love, laughter, and countless more Instagram-worthy moments with my one and only. 📷 💏 #LoveOfMyLife #ForeverYours #FairyTaleRomance #PatiencePaysOff

Arya smirked satirically at the post. Though not really close, she had known Shrithi for a long time now and was contemplating what the post should have actually read:

🙄 ✦ Thrilled to share that in my extensive three-week quest for eternal love, I've miraculously stumbled upon my "forever" for the fourth time! 💞 🔁 ✦ Who needs consistency, am I right? 🤷 The universe must've had a scheduling hiccup, but hey, destiny works in mysterious ways, right? 😄 🌙 To those who think love is a patient waiting game, let me tell you, my love life is on a fast track. 🚀 🔭 Here's to hoping my newfound "forever" lasts longer than my previous three forevers combined. 🤞 🍀 #SerialMonogamist #FastTrackRomance #LoveOnSpeedDial #ForeversComeAndGo

Ah, the enchanting realm of social media, where lives are filtered to perfection, and reality is but a distant acquaintance. How marvellous! Except, do we ever see the behind-the-scenes struggle of #goldenhour to get that one Insta-worthy shot without squinting into the sun?

And then, the #HomeChefExtraordinaire, whose culinary creations appear straight out of a Michelin-starred restaurant. Bravo! But who captures the chaos in the kitchen, the burnt offerings sacrificed to the culinary gods before that one aesthetically pleasing dish emerged?

Oh, the #FitnessGurus sculpting their bodies into Greek statues, sharing daily workout routines that put Olympians to shame. Admirable! Yet, the untold saga of the discarded gym memberships, the abandoned diets, and the midnight snack rendezvous elude the spotlight.

Let's not forget the #WanderlustWanderers, documenting exotic adventures in far-off lands. Mesmerizing! But who captures the lost luggage sagas, the navigational mishaps, or the less-than-glamorous moments when the hotel room doesn't match the brochure?

In this curated universe, everyone seems to have it all – the dream job, the perfect relationship, the flawless skin, the gourmet meals, the sculpted physique, and the jet-setting lifestyle. It's a parade of picture-perfect lives, meticulously staged for the digital audience.

Aarya felt the pressure mounting, as if her phone screen was taunting her with a virtual "tick-tock" sound. The satirical voice in her head piped up, "Attention, Aarya! You're falling behind on the Life Achievement Bingo. Quick, find a partner, a mortgage, and a vegetable garden, or you'll miss out on the grand prize—a lifetime supply of envy from your peers!"

Aarya sighed, contemplating the cosmic irony that her timeline was more synchronized than a Swiss watch, while her own life resembled a chaotic symphony played by tone-deaf musicians. She couldn't escape the feeling that she was running late for some unseen deadline, a deadline dictated by society's unwritten rules.

In the midst of this virtual chaos, Aarya's thumb hovered over the deactivate button. The allure of a life without the constant barrage of curated happiness and #relationshipgoals seemed tempting. But then, what would she do during those awkward elevator rides or the long queues at the grocery store?

A satirical voice in her head chimed in, "Congratulations, Aarya! You've successfully completed Level 27 of Adulting—oh wait, you haven't bought a house yet? Shame on you!"

Aarya chuckled at the thought. Perhaps her life wasn't a checklist, and maybe, just maybe, her happiness didn't have to come with a timestamp. After all, who needed a relationship status when you could have a thriving collection of cat memes?

And so, Aarya's thumb retreated from the deactivate button, and she decided to face the onslaught of success stories, relationship updates, and cat videos head-on. After all, life's timeline might be a tangled web of virtual achievements, but Aarya was determined to navigate it with a healthy dose of humour and a pinch of sarcasm. Little did she know, the adventure had just begun.

CHAPTER 2

THE UNWELCOME ECHOES OF THE PAST

Aarya's apartment, a haven of warmth and familiarity, basked in the soft glow of the evening light that filtered through the curtains. The cozy ambiance was complemented by the inviting embrace of her well-worn couch, where she found solace after a long day. Engrossed in the comforting world of a Bollywood rom-com playing on the screen, she surrendered to the whimsical allure of a narrative where love triumphed over all.

As the plot reached a crescendo, and the hero prepared to spill his heart out, the tranquillity of her movie night was abruptly interrupted by the insistent trill of her smartphone. Startled out of the cinematic reverie, she reluctantly tore her gaze away from the screen to find her phone lighting up with the unmistakable caller ID – "Mom."

With a resigned sigh, Aarya navigated the sea of cushions to retrieve her phone, contemplating the impending conversation. As she swiped to answer, she braced herself for the familiar series of questions that awaited – an annual interrogation into the intricacies of her life, the elusive search for love, and the unrelenting inquiry that echoed through the phone: "When are you getting married?" The cinematic romance would have to make way for the real-life drama of a conversation with her well-meaning but persistently curious mother.

"Hello, Aarya!" her mom's voice, filled with warmth, greeted her. "How are you doing?"

"I'm good, Mom. Just catching up on some movies. What's up?" Aarya replied, trying to sound casual despite the anticipation of the impending inquisition.

"Well, you won't believe what I heard today," her mom said with a tone that suggested this was no ordinary piece of news.

Aarya braced herself. If it was about another distant relative's son getting engaged, she'd heard enough for a lifetime. "What is it, Mom?"

"Latha aunty was here earlier, you know, the one from next door with the ever-watchful eyes," her mom began, causing Aarya's stomach to churn. She groaned inwardly. Latha aunty was the neighbourhood's unofficial gossip queen, armed with binoculars and a radar for sniffing out everyone's business. She was a character Aarya secretly detested. "What did she have to say now?"

Her mom chuckled, "You won't believe it. She claims Aashish is getting married!"

Aarya's heart skipped a beat. Aashish, her childhood playmate, the one everyone teasingly predicted would be her future husband. She hadn't thought about him in a while, and the news felt like an unwelcome blast from the past. "Wait, what? Aashish? Married?"

"Yes, and not just to anyone. He's marrying Isha, Mr. Gopalan's daughter," her mom revealed.

Aarya's mind raced to process the information. Aashish, the guy who had always been in the background of her life, was now tying the knot with the heir to a traditional Indian snacks empire. The scenario seemed surreal, like a page ripped out of a childhood notebook that had been carelessly thrown into the present.

"Isn't Isha the girl from the snacks stores across India? The one who's supposed to inherit the entire business?" Aarya asked, trying to piece together the fragments of this unexpected puzzle.

"The very same. Latha aunty says it's going to be a grand affair, a union of families and businesses," her mom explained.

Aarya couldn't help but feel a pang of nostalgia mixed with discomfort. The childhood jokes about her and Aashish getting married had always seemed silly, a playful jest that held no weight. But now, with the news of his impending marriage, those echoes of the past reverberated in her mind.

"Interesting turn of events, isn't it?" her mom commented, sensing Aarya's contemplative silence.

"Yeah, interesting is one way to put it," Aarya replied, her thoughts a whirlwind of memories and emotions.

After hanging up with her mom, Aarya found herself lost in a cascade of recollections. Aashish, the boy who had been a constant in her life, had evolved from a childhood companion to a kind of ex-boyfriend—a label that felt both ambiguous and unsettling.

Their friendship had taken an unexpected turn when Aashish had confessed his feelings for Aarya during their college days. It had been an unwelcome revelation for her, a disruption to the comfortable familiarity of their dynamic. Aarya's reaction, laced with awkwardness and an unintentional harshness, had cast a shadow over their friendship, turning it into a realm of unspoken sentiments.

The satirical voice in Aarya's head resurfaced, "Congratulations, Aarya! You've just stumbled upon the 'Kind of Ex-Files' chapter. Now, can you navigate the maze of mixed emotions without getting lost in the memories of what could have been?"

Aarya, torn between the past and the present, decided to indulge in some social media exploration. She found herself scrolling through Aashish's profile, the virtual window into his life. The engagement photos with Isha portrayed a narrative of tradition, opulence, and the promise of a shared future.

As Aarya scrolled through the images, she couldn't help but notice the genuine happiness in Aashish's eyes. The playful glint that she had known since childhood now danced in a new context. The congratulatory comments flooded the post, creating a digital tapestry of well-wishes for the couple.

The satirical voice teased, "Well, Aarya, it seems you're about to embark on a journey through the 'Kind of Ex-Files Reloaded.' Are you ready to witness the digital saga of a childhood playmate turned husband-to-be?"

Caught in a whirlwind of emotions, Aarya debated whether, if invited, attending the wedding was a gesture of goodwill or a plunge into a sea of unresolved sentiments. She felt the weight of history and the unspoken words between them, wondering if this grand event could bridge the gap that had silently grown between them over the years.

As Aarya continued to navigate the uncharted territory of her kind-of-ex's impending wedding, she realized that life's twists and turns were indeed unpredictable. The echoes of childhood predictions had evolved into a complex present, and Aarya had to decide whether to embrace the nostalgia, confront the awkwardness, or gracefully bow out of the unexpected drama.

With a deep breath and a thoughtful gaze, Aarya stepped into the next phase of this unexpected narrative, ready to unravel the threads of her past and present.

Calling "Meera"!

MEERA'S CANVAS OF INFLUENCE

The soft hum of the ceiling fan echoed in Aarya's small apartment as she dialled Meera's number. The phone rang a few times before Meera's cheerful voice filled the line. "Hey, Aarya! What's up?"

Aarya, her mind swirling with thoughts of Aashish's impending wedding, decided to divert her attention and dive into the vibrant world of Meera's life. "Nothing much, just thought of catching up. How's the glamorous life of an influencer treating you?"

Meera laughed, the sound echoing through the phone. "Oh, you know, the usual. But hey, I'm always ready for a chat with my favourite realist. What's on your mind?"

Aarya sighed, the weight of her thoughts lifting with Meera's infectious enthusiasm. "Okay, spill it. What's the latest and greatest in the world of Meera?"

Meera took a theatrical breath. "Well, the latest is that I've just partnered with a high-end fashion brand for a collaboration. Can you believe it? They actually want my opinions on fashion!"

Aarya chuckled, her skepticism evident. "Opinions on fashion? Meera, you lived in your pajamas for an entire week last month."

Meera giggled. "True, but I've got a flair for comfort. Pajamas are the unsung heroes of fashion, you know."

Aarya couldn't help but smile. Meera, with her carefree spirit and unconventional approach to life, was a breath of fresh air in Aarya's world. "So, when's the fashion show?"

"Oh, it's all virtual, you know, considering the times we live in. But I'll be creating some amazing content, and the best part—I get to keep all the clothes!" Meera exclaimed.

The satirical voice in Aarya's head joined the conversation, "Congratulations, Meera! You've just unlocked the 'Virtual Runway' achievement. Now, can you convince Aarya that fashion is more than just finding the comfiest pair of pajamas?"

Aarya shook her head with a playful grin. "Alright, Fashion Guru Meera, teach me your ways. But, in all seriousness, I'm happy for you. It's great that you're doing what you love."

Meera's tone shifted, becoming more sincere. "Thanks, Aarya. You know, it's not just about fashion for me. It's about expressing myself, creating art, and connecting with people. It's like my canvas, and I get to paint it the way I want."

Aarya respected Meera's fervour for the digital realm, even though she struggled to fully comprehend the magnetic appeal of the virtual canvas. In Aarya's eyes, Meera was a trailblazer navigating the uncharted territories of the online world with unwavering enthusiasm. The passion Meera exhibited for her digital pursuits was evident in every meticulously crafted post, every strategically timed hashtag, and every artfully edited photo that adorned her social media profiles.

For Aarya, the charm of Meera's virtual adventures remained somewhat elusive. While Meera revelled in the symphony of likes, comments, and shares, Aarya found herself standing on the outskirts of this digital carnival, observing with a mix of bemusement and bemusement. The intricacies of trending hashtags, influencer collaborations, and the algorithmic dance that dictated online visibility were a perplexing labyrinth that Aarya hesitated to tread.

Yet, amid the bemusement, Aarya recognized the significance of Meera's digital endeavours. Meera wasn't merely navigating social media; she was shaping narratives, influencing trends, and carving out a unique space for herself in the vast expanse of the internet. Despite their differing perspectives on the virtual canvas, Aarya admired Meera's ability to harness the power of the online world and recognized that, in this era, it was a language worth understanding, even if it seemed to be written in emojis and hashtags.

"I get that. It's just a little hard for me to wrap my head around the whole influencer thing. I mean, when we were kids, we didn't dream of becoming influencers, did we?"

Meera's voice softened. "No, we didn't. But dreams evolve, Aarya. Life takes unexpected turns. Speaking of which, what's going on with you? You sound a bit off."

Aarya hesitated, debating whether to unload her thoughts about Aashish's impending wedding on Meera. Meera had always been her confidante, someone who understood the complexities of Aarya's emotions. "It's Aashish. He's getting married to Isha, Mr. Gopalan's daughter."

Meera's silence spoke volumes. Aarya could almost feel her friend processing the information. Finally, Meera spoke, "That's quite a bombshell. How are you handling it?"

"I don't know, Meera. It's just weird. I never imagined he'd end up with someone like her. It's like I'm living in some alternate reality," Aarya admitted, her voice tinged with a mix of confusion and nostalgia.

Meera's empathy radiated through the phone. "You know, relationships are like paintings. Sometimes, the artist chooses unexpected colours, and the canvas turns into something entirely different. Aashish is painting his canvas, and so are you. It's okay to feel a bit disoriented."

Aarya sighed, grateful for Meera's wisdom. "Thanks, Mother Meera! You always have a way of putting things into perspective."

Meera chuckled. "Well, that's what the 'Relationship Guru' is here for. Speaking of which, tell me more about this wedding. Are you invited?"

"Well, he hasn't sent me an invitation yet. But I don't think it will be long before I get one!" Aarya replied, still processing the surreal nature of the situation.

Meera's tone took on a mischievous note. "You know what this means, right? It's time to unleash the ultimate outfit. We're talking about a dress that says, 'I'm fabulous, and I know it.'"

Aarya couldn't help but laugh. "You're unbelievable, Meera. I don't know if I can pull off 'fabulous' at a wedding."

Meera countered, "Oh, please! You're gorgeous, Aarya. We just need to find the right outfit to showcase that."

As the conversation shifted to fashion, Aarya felt a sense of relief. Meera, with her boundless energy and unwavering support, had a knack for turning the mundane into an adventure. They discussed potential outfits, fashion trends, and even debated the merits of virtual runways versus traditional catwalks.

The satirical voice chimed in once again, "Congratulations, Aarya! You've just unlocked the 'Fashionista in the Making' achievement. Now, can you attend a wedding without accidentally spilling something on your fabulous outfit?"

Aarya couldn't help but smile. Meera, with her quirky approach to life, had successfully diverted her mind from the complexities of relationships and the impending wedding. As they continued to chat about fashion, dreams, and the ever-evolving canvas of life, Aarya realized how far they had come from where they started off.

In school, Meera was the epitome of glamour and popularity, known as the "Queen Bee". With her striking looks and a trail of admirers, she effortlessly navigated the social scene. Aarya, on the other hand, observed Meera from a distance, marvelling at her fame but assuming they moved in different circles.

One day, at the mall with her friends, Aarya stumbled upon a more vulnerable side of Meera. In the bathroom, she heard soft sobs and was surprised to find Meera, the seemingly unshakable College Queen, in tears. Meera, embarrassed by being caught in a moment of vulnerability, implored Aarya not to reveal her emotional episode to anyone at school. Shocked that Meera even knew her name, Aarya awkwardly promised, and from that day forward, their relationship took an unexpected turn.

Despite Meera's external facade of confidence, Aarya soon discovered the complexities beneath the surface. Meera's parents had just gone through a divorce, and she constantly juggled between two homes, navigating the challenges of a broken family.

In her quest for love, Meera encountered a series of relationships with less-than-desirable individuals. However, amidst the turmoil, one constant remained— her unwavering friendship with Aarya. Their bond, forged in a moment of vulnerability, became a lifeline for Meera, offering stability and solace in the midst of life's unpredictable storms, and for Aarya too.

"Hello?" questioned Meera from the other end of the line. While Aarya collected her thoughts again and responded to her, Meera got a text – Gaurav had news and needed them both! Yet Again!

CHAPTER 4

~~GAURAV~~ GOUHRRAVV

It was an ordinary office party, filled with the usual suspects: the overly enthusiastic interns, the boss trying to dance and failing spectacularly, and of course, Mandana—the snooty, bitchy presence that Aarya couldn't quite shake off. But this party would be different, for it introduced Aarya and Meera to the enigma that was Gaurav, the self-proclaimed woke wonder.

Meera, as usual, accompanied Aarya as her plus one to social events and effortlessly became a crowd favourite. Aarya couldn't help but marvel at how well Meera navigated social gatherings, effortlessly striking up conversations and leaving a lasting impression. Sometimes, Aarya found herself pondering if some of her colleagues mistakenly assumed that Meera was the one employed there, given Aarya's more reserved nature in the workplace. While Aarya preferred to keep a low profile, Meera effortlessly charmed her way into the social circles, becoming a beacon of sociability that Aarya occasionally envied in her quieter moments at work.

Gaurav, on the other hand, made an unexpected appearance as Mandana's guest, catching everyone off guard. Mandana, known for her sharp tongue and love for office drama, seized the opportunity to add a sarcastic twist. "Hey, Aarya, Meera, say hello to Gaurav. He's my plus one for the night. I know, it's a bit surprising, but even the most socially aware and woke individuals need a break from changing the world, don't they?" Mandana's sly remark echoed through the room, leaving Aarya and Meera amused but slightly intrigued by the unexpected pairing.

Aarya exchanged a quick glance with Meera, both wondering what Mandana had in store for them this time. Little did they know that Gaurav would turn out to be a breath of fresh, albeit confusing, air.

Gaurav, with his perfectly coiffed man bun and an array of badges proclaiming his commitment to various social causes, exuded an aura of self-awareness that bordered on the absurd. He greeted Aarya and Meera with an enthusiastic, "Namaste, fellow earthlings! Ready to embark on a journey of consciousness tonight?"

As Aarya tried to stifle a chuckle, Meera couldn't help but give Gaurav a curious once-over. "Consciousness? Is that the new theme for the party, or did I miss the memo?"

Gaurav shook his head, the sincerity in his eyes unmistakable. "Oh, no, no. It's a theme for life. We're all on a cosmic journey, and I'm just here to spread some woke wisdom along the way."

As the conversation unfolded, Aarya and Meera found themselves in the company of a character unlike any they had encountered before. Gaurav seamlessly transitioned from discussing climate change to critiquing the patriarchy, all while sipping on his kale smoothie. Mandana, who had hoped to subtly mock Aarya and Meera by bringing Gaurav into the mix, was left bewildered as Gaurav's infectious enthusiasm charmed the duo.

Over the course of the evening, Gaurav and Aarya discovered a shared passion for dry humour and an uncanny ability to find irony in even the most well-intentioned conversations about social justice. Meanwhile, Mandana's attempts to infiltrate their newfound camaraderie were met with polite nods and barely concealed eye rolls.

As the night unfolded, Gaurav's quest for self-discovery took an unexpected turn. Amid discussions on intersectionality and veganism, he candidly confessed, "You know, witnessing various identity issues worldwide has left me questioning—do I truly understand who I am? Is there more to me than the socially conscious badges I wear?"

Aarya and Meera exchanged amused glances, intrigued by the sudden introspection in the midst of their lively conversation. Unbeknownst to them, Mandana, the office drama aficionado, overheard snippets of their dialogue and seized the opportunity to sow the seeds of chaos.

In the following days, office whispers morphed into elaborate rumours orchestrated by Mandana and her devoted minions. Oblivious to the brewing drama, Aarya unwittingly became the protagonist in a fantastical tale— accused of masterfully stealing Gaurav away from Mandana's anticipated clutches. The office grapevine hummed with stories of Aarya's alleged cunning ways and her supposed plot to snatch Mandana's potential "would be."

In a theatrical flourish, Mandana approached Aarya, feigning exasperation. "Oh, Aarya, you've truly outdone yourself this time. Gaurav was meant to be mine, you know. But alas, you've ensnared him with your devious charm."

Aarya, taken aback by the absurdity of the accusation, exchanged bemused glances with Meera, who had come to drop something off for Aarya. "Gaurav? Seriously? Mandana, you must be joking. We just met him at the party."

Undeterred, Mandana persisted in weaving a tapestry of rumours, casting Aarya as a manipulative enchantress who had lured Gaurav away. Meanwhile, Aarya and Meera decided to confront Gaurav about the brewing chaos. Unbothered, and blissfully oblivious to the storm that had inadvertently sparked, Gaurav opened up about his struggle with identity. "It's a crisis, you know? I've observed so many grappling with it, and now it's my turn. I just want to understand if there's more to me than my woke persona."

Aarya and Meera burst into laughter at Gaurav's earnest revelation, assuring him that his identity crisis was a perfectly normal exploration. Together, they navigated the labyrinth of office gossip and Gaurav's existential musings, solidifying their friendship in the process.

Their chosen haven, a charming coffee shop adorned with fairy lights and the gentle murmur of conversations, became a sanctuary for laughter, discussions that straddled the line between profundity and absurdity, and, of course, the perpetual quest for the perfect cup of coffee.

✳ ✳ ✳

On this particular day, Aarya and Meera found themselves nestled in the cozy corner booth, eagerly awaiting Gaurav's arrival. As the door chimed, Gaurav strolled in, his man bun slightly askew, a kale smoothie in one hand, and an air of intrigue enveloping him.

"Namaste, my fellow conscious beings!" Gaurav greeted, his eyes twinkling with excitement.

Aarya rolled her eyes playfully. "What's with the theatrics today, Gaurav? You look like you're about to drop the hottest woke album of the year."

Meera joined in the banter. "Yeah, spill it. What's the news and Why the grand entrance?"

Gaurav settled into the booth with a flourish, his eyes gleaming with a secret he couldn't wait to share. "Oh, you two, you won't believe what happened. Brace yourselves for the news of the century!"

Aarya and Meera exchanged amused glances, curious about the revelation that seemed to be brewing. Gaurav, taking a theatrical sip of his vegan soy latte that their favourite waiter had ready for him as soon as he arrived, leaned in as if he were about to share classified information.

"So, you remember my early morning laughing club sessions, right?" Gaurav began, his voice a conspiratorial whisper.

Meera chuckled. "The ones where you laugh at the absurdity of life while everyone else is still half-asleep? Hard to forget."

Gaurav nodded with a mysterious air. "Well, during one of those sessions, I met this astrologer cum numerologist. A man of cosmic insights, if you will. He dropped a bombshell that shook the very foundations of my being."

Aarya and Meera exchanged bewildered glances, wondering what revelation could have emerged from Gaurav's laughter-filled rendezvous with an astrologer.

"He hinted," Gaurav continued, "that the way I spell my name could be holding me back in the cosmic dance of life."

Aarya stifled a laugh. "Hold on, Gaurav. Are you telling us that your entire existence hinges on the arrangement of letters in your name?"

Gaurav nodded solemnly. "Indeed. The universe is vast, my friends, and every letter carries cosmic vibrations. The astrologer suggested that a simple alteration in the spelling could unlock untold possibilities."

Meera, ever the pragmatic one, raised an eyebrow. "So, what did you do? Change your name to Gaauraav or something?"

Gaurav grinned, revealing a gleeful glint in his eyes. "Better, my dear Meera. I present to you the new and improved version of myself—Gouhrravv."

Aarya and Meera burst into laughter, unable to contain their amusement at Gaurav's cosmic rebranding. Gaurav, basking in the attention, explained, "The additional 'h' adds a touch of celestial balance, and the extra 'r' symbolize resilience. The 'o' and the 'v' mean something too. It's a cosmic upgrade, my friends."

Aarya, wiping away tears of laughter, quipped, "Gouhrravv, huh? You've truly outdone yourself this time."

Gaurav, undeterred by their laughter, continued, "Laugh all you want, but the astrologer said this cosmic tweak could lead to unexpected revelations. The universe works in mysterious ways, you know."

Meera, with a mischievous glint in her eye, teased, "So, Gouhrravv, what's next? Will the cosmos grant you a lifetime supply of kale smoothies?"

Gaurav, playing along, nodded solemnly. "Ah, the universe works in mysterious ways. Kale smoothies might just be the tip of the cosmic iceberg."

As they kept chatting and enjoying the silliness of Gaurav's deep reflections, they didn't realize that the coffee shop had become a backdrop for a moment of universal comedy. Gaurav, armed with his newfound understanding of himself, delighted in the simple joys of the moment, dancing with the cosmos with a carefree spirit.

Surrounded by the delightful scent of freshly brewed coffee and the contagious sound of laughter, Aarya, Meera, and Gouhrravv stepped into the next phase of their peculiar friendship. They were prepared to confront life's cosmic uncertainties armed with a hearty laugh and an unbreakable bond.

CHAPTER 5

A Late-Night Call and the Unveiling of Rainbows

The night was draped in a quiet hush, and Aarya was happily floating in the world of dreams, where mundane problems didn't exist, and everyone had a pet unicorn. That tranquillity, however, was interrupted by the shrill ringtone of her phone, jolting her from the whimsical utopia.

"Hello?" Aarya croaked, her voice a mix of confusion and morning gruffness.

"Aarya maasi, it's Kriya."

Now, receiving a call from Kriya in the middle of the night was not entirely unusual. Teenagers had this uncanny ability to conduct clandestine operations under the cover of darkness. However, the tone of Kriya's voice suggested this was no ordinary covert mission.

With a sudden burst of alertness, Aarya sat up in bed, switching on the bedside lamp. "Kriya, what's wrong? Is everything okay?"

And then came the bombshell, delivered in the most unexpected fashion: "Aarya maasi, I think I might be gay."

The words hung in the air, daring Aarya to react. She blinked, processing the revelation while contemplating the possibility of accidentally entering a parallel universe in her sleep-deprived state.

In the dim light of her room, Aarya leaned against the headboard, silently willing strength into her words. She had been a pillar of support for Kriya since Asha, Aarya's beloved cousin and Kriya's mother, lost her battle to cancer three years ago. Aarya became the maternal figure that Kriya desperately needed during her formative years.

As Kriya opened up about her thoughts and feelings, Aarya listened intently, absorbing the complexities of Kriya's emotions. The night transformed into a space of vulnerability, where truths were spoken and confessions shared.

"Aarya maasi, are you there?" Kriya's voice wavered.

Aarya snapped back to reality. "Yes, yes! I'm here. Sorry, just processing.

"Aarya maasi, I miss Mom so much. I wish she were here to guide me through this," Kriya admitted, her voice tinged with longing.

Aarya's heart ached for Kriya, and she felt a profound sense of loss for Asha, a woman who had been a sister, a confidante, and a dear friend. "I miss her too, sweetheart. Your mom was incredible, and I know she would have embraced and supported you through anything. But remember, you have me. I'm here for you, no matter what."

Aarya continued, "Now, let me tell you something important: I love you, no matter what. And if you're wondering whether you've reached the wrong number and dialled your friendly neighbourhood superhero instead, you haven't. I'm here for you, cape and all."

The conversation unfolded into a comedic yet heartfelt exchange. As Kriya poured out her heart, Aarya offered a mix of sage advice and humour. "Sweetie, discovering your true self is like trying to find matching socks in the laundry. It takes time, but you eventually get there, and it's oddly satisfying."

As the conversation unfolded, Aarya found herself navigating uncharted waters. She had always been the reliable anchor for Kriya, but this was uncharted territory for both of them. Yet, Aarya's love for Kriya transcended any uncertainty. She was determined to provide the support Kriya needed, even if it meant embarking on this journey together.

Days turned into nights, and the duo's conversations evolved into a sitcom of self-discovery. They binged on LGBTQ+ resources, attended local support groups, and Aarya, with a newfound commitment, educated herself on everything from rainbows to acronyms that seemed to multiply faster than rabbits.

In the midst of conversations about sexual orientation and identity, Aarya couldn't help but marvel at Kriya's resilience and courage. "You're like a superhero with a rainbow cape, Kriya. I can see it now: The Unveiling of Rainbows, coming soon to theatres near you."

Kriya chuckled, "Can I have a sidekick named Chroma-Confusion?"

Aarya burst into laughter, "Absolutely! And together, we'll conquer the world, one colourful revelation at a time."

Kriya looked at Aarya with gratitude in her eyes. "Maasi, I'm so lucky to have you. Thank you for being my guiding star through all of this." Aarya embraced Kriya, a silent promise in the warmth of that hug—a promise to navigate the rainbow together, to cherish the beauty of identity, and to stand resilient in the face of uncertainties.

CHAPTER 6

THE GENDER/IDENTITY EXTRAVAGANZA

As Aarya navigated the vast ocean of information on Kriya's journey, she stumbled upon a peculiar online universe where gender and identity discussions had taken a nosedive into the realm of the ludicrous. Brace yourself, dear reader, for a satirical journey through the looking glass.

In one corner of the internet, Aarya stumbled upon discussions on Gender. Aarya still held the view that there were primarily two genders: Men with male reproductive parts and Women with female reproductive parts. The nuances of gender identification intrigued her, prompting a surge of curiosity within.

In the midst of discussions about gender identity, Aarya found herself in a tornado of debates that left her more puzzled than enlightened. The world appeared to be grappling with new ideas and terms, creating a confusing landscape. Pronouns, non-binary expressions, and a spectrum of identities were now part of everyday conversations, making it feel like understanding a foreign language without a guide.

As Aarya listened to these conversations, she couldn't shake the feeling that things were getting complicated rather than clearer. Instead of breaking down old systems, the discussions seemed to be adding layers to them. The patriarchal society, far from diminishing, was adapting and using the complexity of these discussions to its advantage. Aarya struggled to see the true direction of progress. Were we moving towards real equality, or was it just a show? The more she tried to understand, the more it seemed like the world was replacing simplicity with complexity. The debates and the stories of seized opportunities, instead of bringing clarity, created a confusing web of labels that made it hard to see the path to genuine equality.

As Aarya thought about these things, she wondered if the world was trading straightforwardness for confusion. In the attempt to break free from old norms, it seemed like society was building a maze where the journey to equality was obscured by the very terms meant to help. The debate, which was supposed to lead to progress, now felt like a puzzle wrapped in mystery.

In another corner of the internet, she stumbled upon "personal identification" crises. Aarya found people proudly claiming their allegiance to the animal kingdom. "Woof! I'm Fido, a dog stuck in a human's body. Fetch me a bone, will you?" These declarations were accompanied by profile pictures of humans wearing dog ears and tails. Aarya wondered if they had secret doggy treat stashes hidden in their closets.

The absurdity reached new heights when she encountered a woman who decided to embark on a literal blind date with destiny. In an act that could only be described as eye-rolling, she deliberately poured some mysterious concoction into her eyes, all in the pursuit of identifying as a blind person. Aarya couldn't decide if this was performance art or just a misguided attempt to see life from a different perspective.

The madness didn't stop at the online realm. Schools had become the battleground for the next generation's identity revolution. Show-and-tell sessions turned into showcases of creativity gone wild. "Meet Susie, she identifies as a toaster, and she's poppin' with uniqueness!" announced the teacher, as Susie stood there with a cardboard box painted to resemble a toaster.

Parents, evidently, were embracing their role as supporters of their children's peculiar identity choices. PTA meetings became surreal gatherings where moms and dads fervently discussed their newfound allegiances. "My little Timmy identifies as a stapler, and we couldn't be prouder. It's so "staplingly" progressive!" gushed one enthusiastic parent.

Amidst the chaos, Aarya found herself at a crossroads. On one hand, she recognized the importance of meaningful discussions about sexual orientations and identities. On the other hand, she was wary of diving headfirst into the absurdities that seemed to have hijacked the conversation.

In the end, Aarya chose a path of enlightenment rather than eccentricity. She decided to embrace the meaningful discussions, the stories of courage and acceptance, and leave the absurdities at the door. As she closed the virtual door on people identifying as sentient staplers and intentionally blindfolded individuals, Aarya took a deep breath, ready to explore the depths of understanding without drowning in the sea of absurdity. After all, there was a fine line between celebrating diversity and identifying as a walking, talking, human-sized toaster.

CHAPTER 7

THE MIDNIGHT TAMPON TANGO

The clock struck an ungodly hour, and Aarya, usually tucked into the cozy embrace of sleep, found herself rudely awakened by a sudden bout of paranoia. In the hazy blur between dreams and reality, a singular thought seized her: had she, by any chance, forgotten to bid adieu to her tampon from two nights ago?

Panic set in as Aarya, wrapped in the suffocating darkness of her room, tried to rewind the mental tape of her bathroom escapades. In the silence of the night, she pondered the cosmic possibilities of an MIA tampon wandering around her insides like a misplaced sock in the laundry.

The night unfolded like a quirky quest into the unfamiliar terrain of feminine hygiene mishaps. Aarya's fingers danced across the keyboard, typing questions one wouldn't dare utter in broad daylight. "Can a tampon disappear?" and "Is my uterus a tampon hide-and-seek champion?" were among the gems she tossed into the vast sea of internet wisdom.

The search results resembled a carnival of conflicting opinions, each more bizarre than the last. From conspiracy theories about tampon teleportation to horror tales of forgotten tampons triggering global cataclysms, Aarya found herself teetering on the brink of hysteria.

As she navigated through YouTube tutorials on DIY tampon retrieval techniques and read testimonials that ranged from humorous to downright alarming, Aarya's sense of impending doom intensified. The glow of her screen became a portal to a parallel universe where tampons held the power to unleash cosmic chaos.

The clock's relentless ticking echoed her growing anxiety, each second amplifying the gravity of her nocturnal tampon conundrum. Little did Aarya know that this digital escapade would soon transcend the virtual realm, dragging her into the real-life arena of feminine mystique.

Aarya couldn't bear the uncertainty any longer. Armed with determination and fuelled by the fear of forgotten tampons, she stormed into the bathroom. There, with the urgency of a detective on a high-stakes case, she scrubbed her hands with soap, preparing for the archaeological expedition into the unknown depths. As if excavating for a lost city, she delved into the recesses of her own body, hoping to unearth the elusive tampon. Alas, her quest proved fruitless, and panic set in. In a desperate attempt to decode her own anatomy, she turned to the internet, seeking guidance on the female body like a bewildered explorer lost in a jungle of uncertainty.

Feeling like an unwitting participant in a midnight comedy of errors, Aarya decided she needed a sanity check. She dialled Meera's number, fully aware that no reasonable conversation ever happened at this hour.

"Meera, wake up. I'm in a crisis," Aarya blurted out the moment Meera answered the call.

Meera, with a distinct mix of annoyance and curiosity in her voice, replied, "Do you realize it's 3 AM? Did you finally come to terms with your fear of the dark?"

Aarya, her voice a symphony of panic, retorted, "No, it's worse. I may have forgotten to remove my tampon from two nights ago. I dug around my holy chamber like a friggin' archaeologist but I feel nothing! "

There was a moment of silence on the other end, and then Meera burst into laughter, the kind that echoes through the quiet of the night like a rebellious rooster in a silent town.

"Aarya, only you could turn a midnight crisis into a comedy. Did the tampon sprout legs and make a run for it?"

Aarya groaned, "Meera, this is serious. I could be harbouring a renegade tampon, and I need help. What if it's planning a coup inside me?"

Amused by the absurdity of the situation, Meera suggested, "Maybe it's building a tiny fort in there, complete with a moat of menstrual blood."

As the banter continued, Aarya and Meera decided that a pilgrimage to the gynaecologist was in order. In the eerie stillness of the night, they embarked on a mission to uncover the truth behind the potential tampon insurgency.

As they waited in the gynaecologist's office, Meera couldn't resist weaving tales of the tampon's nocturnal adventures. "Maybe it's moonlighting as a superhero. Tampon Woman, defender of uteruses everywhere!"

Aarya, a mix of laughter and exasperation, responded, "Meera, this is not the time for superhero fantasies. We need to face the tampon truth."

The gynaecologist, a beacon of calm in the storm of midnight tampon turmoil, ushered Aarya into the examination room. As the clock on the wall ticked away, the doctor calmly assured Aarya that everything would be sorted out.

"I'm going to perform a quick examination," the doctor explained, "and we'll see if we can locate the elusive tampon. Just relax, Aarya."

Easy for the doctor to say. As the examination commenced, Aarya couldn't help but feel like a character in a surreal late-night sitcom, caught in a situation that blurred the lines between hilarity and mortification.

Outside the examination room, Meera entertained herself with an imaginary play-by-play commentary of the tampon expedition. "And here we have Aarya, bravely venturing into the abyss of her uterus. Will she find the tampon or stumble upon the lost city of Atlantis?"

Inside the room, Aarya's mind raced through the possibilities. What if the tampon had become a nocturnal nomad, a wandering soul in the labyrinth of her reproductive system?

Finally, the doctor spoke, "Aarya, I've found the tampon. Crisis averted."

Aarya let out a sigh of relief, feeling a mixture of embarrassment and gratitude. "Thank you, Doctor. And thank you for not turning this into a midnight soap opera. I don't think I could handle the suspense."

As Aarya emerged from the examination room, Meera couldn't contain her laughter. "So, did they find the tampon insurgent?"

Aarya nodded, her face flushed. "It's been located and neutralized. The midnight tampon tango has come to an end."

Meera grinned. "Well, that's one for the midnight memoirs, isn't it? By the way, how did that feel? Taking a stroll into the unexplored, where no fellow has ventured before – the daring journey to the land of untouched experiences", she said, hinting at Aarya still being a virgin at the age of 28.

"Well, I can say, after that little one-on-one with the speculum, for the foreseeable future, nothing is going in or coming out of there. No Trespassing!"

Both the girls burst out into laughter.

CHAPTER 8

THE ODYSSEY OF MISS TIMING

In the quaint town where Aarya grew up, where the picket fences were as judgmental as everyone else in the town, Aarya found herself at the crossroads of love and, well, more crossroads. It all began in the hallowed halls of her high school, an institution known more for its obsession with GPA than teenage romance.

As a studious teenager with a penchant for acing exams, Aarya's mantra was firmly entrenched in the gospel of 'Books before Boys' and 'Grades before Gazing into Dreamy Eyes'. Her classmates, who were busy passing notes with hearts instead of equations, couldn't fathom why Aarya wasn't entangled in the web of adolescent love.

"You know, Aarya, high school is the time to make unforgettable memories," her friend Meena once declared while expertly twirling her hair around her finger. "And by unforgettable memories, I mean sneaking out to meet your crush, not burying your head in textbooks."

Aarya, nose buried in a physics book, replied with her signature eyeroll. "I'm making unforgettable memories with Newton and Einstein. They don't break hearts, just laws of motion."

Meena chuckled, "Well, when you're solving equations, I hope you find the X that represents a love life."

And so, high school passed like a breeze, leaving Aarya with a diploma in one hand and a blank relationship slate in the other. But fear not, for college was the next grand arena where Cupid might unleash his arrows.

Her university, a haven for academia and, apparently, romance according to every rom-com ever made, welcomed Aarya into its hallowed halls. Dormitories buzzed with whispers of love stories in the making, secret admirers, and clandestine rendezvous in the library.

"You've got to loosen up, Aarya," her roommate, Riya, insisted. "College is the time to live a little, maybe even fall in love."

Aarya, engrossed in her thesis on quantum physics, barely looked up. "I'm trying to make my mark in the academic world, not the relationship drama world."

Riya sighed, "You're missing out on the essence of college life – the drama, the intrigue, the heartbreak."

Aarya's college years passed with flying colours, both academically and in steadfast avoidance of any romantic entanglements. She graduated summa cum laude and magna cum abstinence. The once blank relationship slate now sported a zero.

And so, armed with degrees and a pocketful of missed opportunities, Aarya stepped into the professional world, where love stories allegedly bloomed faster than coffee machines on Monday mornings.

At her first job, where spreadsheets were mightier than swords, Aarya became the undisputed queen of data analysis. Colleagues whispered about office romances, secret rendezvous in the supply closet, and stolen glances during meetings. Aarya, however, remained blissfully unaware of this romantic undercurrent, her attention devoted solely to pie charts and pivot tables.

Her co-worker, Rahul, tried his best to break through Aarya's professional armour. "You know, Aarya, we make a great team. Maybe we could be more than just colleagues."

Aarya, eyes fixed on her computer screen, responded with her trademark deadpan humour. "Rahul, the only 'more' I'm interested in right now is more accurate data."

Life unfolded like a scripted comedy, with Aarya dodging Cupid's arrows like a pro. Her friends, now married with children and white picket fences, couldn't fathom how Aarya had managed to elude love for so long.

"You've had three chances, Aarya – high school, college, and now work. How is it that you're still not in love?" Meena asked during a reunion, her toddler clinging to her leg.

Aarya shrugged, "I've been busy building my career. Love can wait."

Meena exchanged an amused glance with the other friends. "Aarya, we built our careers too, but we also built families. When will you let love into your life?"

And so, at the age of 28, Aarya found herself in the crossfire of love anecdotes and romantic escapades. Her nieces and nephews regaled her with tales of first crushes, awkward kisses, and teenage heartbreaks.

"Come on, Aunt Aarya, you must have a crazy love story too," her teenage niece, Vidya, insisted.

Aarya chuckled, "My crazy love story involves me, my laptop, and a passionate affair with data analysis."

As Aarya listened to the laughter and tales of teenage romance from her nieces and nephews, she couldn't help but feel a pang of introspection. Amidst the humorous anecdotes and playful teasing about her supposed "crazy love story" with data analysis, a seed of truth sprouted in the recesses of her mind. Deep down, Aarya knew that the narrative of prioritizing her career over love was a well-constructed facade, a story she had told herself and others for years.

In the solitude of her thoughts, Aarya reflected on the moments that shaped her seemingly love-resistant journey. It wasn't that she hadn't encountered opportunities for romance – the gentle flirtations in high school, the camaraderie with college mates, and the subtle advances at work. Each time, however, as the prospect of connection loomed on the horizon, Aarya instinctively fortified the walls around her heart.

The truth was more complex than the image she projected. Aarya wasn't averse to love; she was afraid of it. The idea of committing to someone, of allowing another person to navigate the intricate corridors of her emotions, sent a shiver down her spine. It wasn't a lack of desire but rather a fear of vulnerability, a fear of relinquishing the control she had meticulously maintained over her life.

In her early years, Aarya had witnessed relationships unravelling around her – friends consumed by the flames of passion that eventually turned to ashes, leaving scars that lingered long after the fire had extinguished. The spectre of heartbreak haunted Aarya, a silent reminder that love wasn't always the idyllic narrative spun in fairy tales.

As high school romances blossomed around her, Aarya chose the safety of her textbooks and the sanctuary of equations. It wasn't that she lacked the capacity to feel; it was her uncanny ability to compartmentalize emotions, locking away the vulnerabilities that love could expose. Each missed opportunity became a brick in the fortress she erected around her heart, a fortress that grew stronger with every passing year.

College, with its reputation as a breeding ground for love stories, presented Aarya with choices that she deliberately sidestepped. Casual flings and carefree dalliances seemed like turbulent waters to someone accustomed to the calm of academic pursuits. Amidst the whirlwind of romance, Aarya clung to the familiarity of her textbooks, seeking refuge in the solace of knowledge rather than the uncertainties of the heart.

Work, with its promise of professional success, provided another convenient excuse to avoid the complexities of love. Colleagues and acquaintances attempted to scale the walls Aarya had built, but she adeptly deflected their advances with a combination of humour and deflection. Her dedication to her career became not only a shield against potential heartbreak but also a shield against confronting the deeper fears that lurked within.

The fear of losing control, of exposing her vulnerabilities, became the silent orchestrator of Aarya's romantic narrative. Behind the facade of indifference was a woman who yearned for connection but couldn't fathom surrendering the carefully curated independence she had cultivated over the years.

As the nieces and nephews giggled about their crushes and first loves, Aarya couldn't escape the realization that, deep inside, she craved those experiences too. The wall she had built, brick by brick, wasn't a testament to her lack of desire for love; it was a monument to her fear of the unknown, a fear that had become an uninvited lodger in the chambers of her heart.

Perhaps it was the fear of vulnerability, the fear of being seen in all her imperfections, that held Aarya captive. Each time love knocked on her door, she pretended not to be home, retreating further into the fortress of logic and reason she had constructed.

But as she listened to the laughter and joy around her, Aarya couldn't ignore the subtle yearning that whispered beneath the surface. The question lingered – was it too late to dismantle the fortress and allow the echoes of love to penetrate her carefully guarded heart?

A whimsical thought crossed her mind – could she craft her own endearing K-drama storyline? Imagining herself in a romantic escapade filled with charming protagonists, captivating plot twists, and perhaps a serendipitous encounter, she couldn't help but entertain the idea of a love story unfolding against the backdrop of her chaotic life. With a mischievous grin, she toyed with the notion of turning her everyday dramas into a scripted narrative, complete with swoon-worthy moments and the promise of a happily ever after.

CHAPTER 9

THE HEART THAT LEAPT AND THE GLITCH THAT HAUNTED

In the vast digital expanse of social media, where every scroll was a journey into the lives of others, Aarya found herself in a moment of digital distress. As she cursorily glided over Aashish's profile for the fifty-first time, a cascade of accidental clicks sent her spiralling into a realm of social media mishaps that would become the epicentre of her mortification.

It all began innocently enough, or so Aarya thought. A simple scroll, a nonchalant traverse through the digital scrapbook of Aashish's life. The photographs, the captions – a mosaic of moments frozen in pixels. Little did Aarya know that this seemingly routine exploration would evolve into a catastrophic journey through the land of accidental likes and technological tantrums.

In her habitual scrolling, Aarya's thumb, guided by fate or perhaps a cruel digital deity, landed on the heart icon beneath a picture from Aashish's recent vacation. Panic gripped her like a vice as the crimson heart glowed on the screen, broadcasting her unintentional admiration to Aashish's notifications.

The world seemed to halt for Aarya. In her desperate attempt to undo the like before Aashish noticed, she frantically stabbed at the heart icon, initiating a comical dance of like and unlike that would have made any seasoned social media user cringe. But Aarya, caught in the vortex of panic, was oblivious to the digital chaos she was orchestrating.

With a sigh of relief, she managed to click 'unlike' on the picture, only to be met with a sinking realization – she had immediately clicked 'like' again, as if the universe itself conspired against her. The heart, now pulsating with a rhythm that matched Aarya's escalating anxiety, seemed to mock her futile attempts at digital subtlety.

In a moment of desperation, Aarya attempted to clear the evidence of her digital fumble. She navigated to Aashish's profile, intending to send a breezy message that would explain the accidental like as a technological glitch. A perfectly reasonable plan, or so it seemed.

As she typed, "Hey Aashish, just casually stumbled onto your profile, and my screen went into this glitch of like and unlike. Blaming it on the technology, you know how it is," Aarya's thumb, still betraying her, clicked on the heart symbol right next to the message, sending Aashish a colossal pounding heart instead of the intended words.

All hell broke loose. Aarya's eyes widened in horror as the digital heart floated across the screen, a virtual declaration of affection that she had neither intended nor felt ready to convey. Aarya, now aghast and frantically attempting damage control, managed to delete the oversized heart, but the universe, evidently not done with its jesting, replaced it with an admin message that hung ominously on the screen – "A message has been deleted."

The technological escapade had unfolded like a tragicomedy, with Aarya at the center of a digital storm of her own making. She could almost hear the echoes of laughter from the digital gods, relishing in the absurdity of the situation.

With a heavy sigh, Aarya considered her options. Retreat and deactivate her account? Perhaps vanish into the digital abyss and emerge under a new pseudonym? As tempting as those thoughts were, Aarya, resilient in her embarrassment, decided to confront the chaos head-on.

Summoning the last shreds of her digital dignity, Aarya composed a straightforward message. "Hey Aashish, sorry about the glitch in my previous message. Damn technology, right? Anyway, how's it going?"

CHAPTER 10

A Comedy of Quirks in the Professional Arena

In the fluorescent-lit labyrinth of her office, where spreadsheets reigned supreme and coffee was the elixir of productivity, Aarya found herself at the intersection of disillusionment and a mid-career crisis. The title of 'Data Analyst' emblazoned on her cubicle felt more like a sentence than an achievement. It wasn't that Aarya hated her job; she just felt like her ambitions had outgrown the confines of data sets and statistical analyses.

Step into the chaotic world of Aarya's office, where balance between work and life is a rare luxury. In this realm, employees are paid a pittance, and the idea of personal time is often ignored. Picture a workplace where success isn't solely about skills but involves navigating tricky office politics. Climbing the corporate ladder is more like a game, where relationships matter more than talent.

In this environment, people work tirelessly, hoping for a better paycheck, but the reality is often disappointing. Loyalty is tested, and the line between personal and professional life blurs. The corporate world can be a challenging place, demanding not only hard work but also an ability to handle the absurdities that unfold.

As Aarya scrutinized the never-ending rows and columns on her screen, Mandana, the resident office nemesis, sauntered over with her signature air of condescension.

"Still crunching numbers, Aarya? Living the dream, I see," Mandana remarked, her voice dripping with sarcasm.

Aarya sighed, keeping her eyes on the screen. "Yes, Mandana, living the dream of unravelling the mysteries of data. What brings you here?"

Mandana leaned against the cubicle partition, a sly grin playing on her lips. "You know, Aarya, there's more to life than Excel sheets and pivot tables. You're wasting your potential here."

Aarya, intrigued despite herself, looked up. "And what, pray tell, is my untapped potential, according to the oracle of Mandana?"

Mandana, revelling in the opportunity to assert her supposed superiority, smirked and proceeded to paint a vivid picture of Aarya as a schemer, strategically stealing away potential partners from her unsuspecting rivals. Aarya, who had been enduring a barrage of condescending remarks and office gossip, finally decided she had had enough. The absurdity of Mandana's claims hit Aarya like a wave of irritation. However, instead of succumbing to the negativity, she mustered the courage to speak her mind.

"Listen, Mandana," Aarya began, her tone firm but not devoid of exasperation. "I don't have the time or energy for these juvenile games. If you want to live in a world where relationships are chess pieces to be moved around, be my guest. But I'm stepping out of this toxic narrative."

Mandana, taken aback by Aarya's sudden assertiveness, attempted to salvage her facade of superiority. "Aarya, you're being so unprofessional right now. This isn't how we handle things in a corporate setting."

Aarya, unfazed, simply responded, "Maybe you're right. This isn't how things are handled in a corporate setting. So, here's my resignation." With that, Aarya handed Mandana a neatly typed letter of resignation, leaving the office drama and toxic dynamics behind. As she walked out, she felt a weight lifting off her shoulders – a step towards freeing herself from the shackles of a toxic workplace.

Little did Aarya know that this impulsive decision would be the catalyst for a new chapter in her life and would spark a comedic odyssey through the wilderness of unconventional career choices.

The Accidental Influencer

In the world of Instagram, where filters disguised imperfections and hashtags held the power of digital sorcery, Aarya embarked on an unintentional journey into the realm of influencing, courtesy of her ever-enthusiastic friend, Meera.

Meera, armed with a phone and a knack for trends, convinced Aarya to embrace the world of influencer culture. "Aarya, you have a unique aesthetic. People will love your insights into the world of data. #DataDiva, that's your brand!"

Reluctantly, Aarya agreed. The next thing she knew, she was sharing posts about the correlation between latte consumption and productivity, complete with aesthetically arranged spreadsheets in the background.

A newfound audience emerged – a mix of confused data enthusiasts and accidental followers who stumbled upon Aarya's quirky journey. Meera's hashtag strategy seemed to work, and Aarya found herself reluctantly embracing the title of 'Influencer Extraordinaire.'

As her following grew, Aarya's Instagram became a haven for data lovers and meme enthusiasts alike. The hashtag #SpreadsheetSundays trended, and Aarya found herself thrust into a digital spotlight she never sought.

Yet, amidst the likes and comments, Aarya couldn't shake the feeling of incongruity. Was this the path she truly wanted to tread, or was she merely a pawn in Meera's grand social media experiment?

The Woke Crusader

Gouhrravv, the self-proclaimed harbinger of enlightenment in Aarya's life, saw potential beyond the confines of influencer aesthetics. He believed Aarya had a responsibility – a duty to awaken the masses to societal injustices and become a woke activist.

"Data isn't just about numbers, Aarya. It's a reflection of society. Use your platform to bring about change," Gouhrravv proclaimed with the zeal of a digital messiah.

And so, Aarya, donning the cape of wokeness, delved into the world of social justice and awareness. Her Instagram feed transformed into a mosaic of infographics, memes, and impassioned pleas for change. The hashtag #WokeDataWarrior became synonymous with Aarya's newfound avatar.

However, as Aarya passionately advocated for causes ranging from climate change to the importance of using gender-neutral emojis, a nagging sense of dissonance crept in. Was this the platform for her true calling, or had she inadvertently become a mouthpiece for Gouhrravv's woke agenda?

The Unlikely Podcaster

As Aarya grappled with the existential crisis of her digital personas, an unexpected twist awaited her on the horizon. During a particularly soul-searching session at a local coffee shop, Gouhrravv proposed a new venture – a podcast that would showcase Aarya's eclectic perspective on life, data, and everything in between.

"Think about it, Aarya. Your voice, your insights – they deserve more than just social media. Let the world hear the wisdom of the Data Diva," Gouhrravv exclaimed, eyes glinting with entrepreneurial fervour.

With trepidation and a hint of curiosity, Aarya agreed. The next thing she knew, she was seated in a booth, headphones on, and a microphone before her. The hashtag #AryasDataDecibels echoed in the digital airwaves.

Surprisingly, the podcast format suited Aarya. The spontaneity, the unfiltered banter, and the freedom to express herself without the constraints of pixels and filters felt liberating. As her show gained traction, Aarya found herself embracing the unexpected role of Podcaster with gusto.

The eclectic mix of topics – from decoding data trends to discussing the existential significance of office plants – resonated with an audience that appreciated Aarya's unique blend of wit and wisdom.

Aarya braced herself as her phone rang, displaying the dreaded caller ID – Latha aunty. The unofficial neighbourhood news channel, Latha aunty had a knack for gathering information faster than Wi-Fi speed. Aarya reluctantly answered, knowing that resistance was futile against the relentless force of her nosy neighbour.

"Hello, Aarya! How have you been?" Latha aunty's voice, a blend of cheerfulness and curiosity, echoed through the phone.

"I'm good, aunty. How are you?" Aarya responded cautiously, fully aware that this casual exchange was merely the calm before the storm of probing questions.

"I heard from your mother that you've changed jobs! Freelance podcasting, is it?" Latha aunty's tone carried a mix of surprise and judgment, as if Aarya had announced a career change to trapeze artist at the circus.

Aarya sighed, mentally preparing for the inevitable interrogation about her career choices, marriage prospects, and the ticking biological clock. "Yes, aunty. I've taken up podcasting. It's something I've always wanted to do."

Silence lingered on the line for a moment, a vacuum waiting to be filled with the unsolicited wisdom of Latha aunty. And then it began – the typical Indian conversation trifecta: career, marriage, and age.

"But Aarya, what about a stable job? And when are you planning to settle down? You know, it's high time you start thinking about these things. Your clock is ticking, and before you know it, you'll be a spinster," Latha aunty chimed in, her concern laden with the weight of societal expectations.

Aarya suppressed an eye roll, having perfected the art of diplomatic responses over the years. "Aunty, I'm happy with my choices. And settling down will happen when it's meant to. I'm just enjoying the journey for now."

But Latha aunty, a seasoned player in the neighbourhood matchmaking game, wasn't one to be easily deterred. The conversation meandered through a maze of unsolicited advice, outdated stereotypes, and well-meaning concern that left Aarya mentally exhausted.

As Latha aunty continued to delve into the intricacies of Aarya's personal and professional life, Aarya couldn't help but wonder if this was a preview of the countless interrogations that awaited her in the grand stage of Indian societal norms. The pressure to conform to age-old expectations, to fit into the neatly carved mould of societal norms, felt suffocating.

In an attempt to maintain her sanity amidst the onslaught of questions, Aarya mastered the art of strategic nods and non-committal responses. Each inquiry was met with a polite deflection, a skill she had honed to perfection over years of navigating through such conversations.

But behind the composed exterior, a storm of frustration and rebellion brewed within Aarya. The expectation to follow a predetermined life script clashed with her desire for autonomy and self-discovery. As Latha aunty delved deeper into the realms of marriage prospects and career stability, Aarya couldn't help but yearn for a world where individual choices were celebrated, not scrutinized.

The conversation, a predictable dance of societal expectations, eventually came to an end. Aarya, mentally drained but outwardly composed, bid Latha aunty farewell with a promise to consider the pearls of wisdom bestowed upon her. Yet, deep down, she knew that her journey was meant to be unique, shaped by her own choices and the pursuit of happiness on her terms.

As she finally hung up, Aarya couldn't help but marvel at the audacity of Latha aunty's inquiries. The dreading phone call had come and gone, leaving in its wake a reminder that societal expectations and nosy neighbours were constants in the chaotic tapestry of Aarya's life.

CHAPTER 11

THE WEDDING COUNTDOWN CONUNDRUM

Aarya stared at her phone screen in disbelief as Aashish's response popped up. Pleasant exchanges about life and work quickly took an unexpected turn when Aashish casually mentioned his upcoming grand three-day wedding extravaganza. Aarya, still processing the information, read the message again to confirm she hadn't misunderstood.

"By the way, Aarya, I'd love for you to be a part of the celebration. It's a three-day affair, and your presence would mean a lot. Looking forward to catching up!"

Aarya's heart skipped a beat. She was being invited to Aashish's wedding – the grand spectacle that had been the talk of the town probably for months. She couldn't deny the mixture of excitement and trepidation that washed over her. The prospect of seeing Aashish after all these years in the midst of a joyous occasion brought a cocktail of emotions.

She hesitated for a moment before composing a carefully crafted response. "Thank you, Aashish! I'd be honoured to attend. Can't wait for the celebration!"

As soon as the virtual ink on her acceptance message dried, reality hit Aarya like a ton of bridal confetti. She was going to a three-day wedding – a cinematic affair that demanded a wardrobe as opulent as the occasion. Aarya, who had mastered the art of online shopping for pajamas and office clothes, found herself faced with the daunting task of choosing outfits fit for a grand celebration.

Enter Meera, the eternal fashion guru and the official relationship sage, who declared Aarya's wardrobe crisis a national emergency. "This is it, Aarya. We're going shopping – a full-fledged field trip to transform you into the belle of the wedding ball!"

Aarya, torn between excitement and the realization that her wardrobe hadn't seen the light of a mall in ages, reluctantly agreed. The duo set off on a mission to conquer the shopping realms, armed with a list of wedding guest essentials and a determination to make Aarya dazzle like never before.

As they stepped into the first store, Aarya felt a twinge of nostalgia mixed with anxiety. The last time she had ventured into a physical store for clothes was a distant memory. Online shopping had become her comfort zone, shielding her from the harsh lighting and judgmental stares of store attendants. Now, faced with an array of vibrant fabrics and sparkling ensembles, Aarya couldn't escape the harsh reality that her size had shifted from the last time she had braved a fitting room.

The revelation struck like a thunderbolt – the M-sized dresses she once flaunted had transformed into XLs. Aarya, a master of data interpretation, questioned reality. "Meera, did brands change their size charts or am I hallucinating?"

Meera, trying to stifle a laugh, responded, "Maybe they did, or maybe it's the universe telling you to embrace the glam XL life. Own it, Aarya!"

But Aarya, lost in a sea of self-doubt, couldn't shake off the harsh reality. She had a wedding to attend, a kind-of ex to impress, and an XL tag to defy. And so, the great wedding weight-off drama unfolded.

The internet became Aarya's weight-loss guru. "How to lose ten kilos in ten days" became her most searched phrase. From celebrity crash diets to bizarre detox rituals, Aarya tried them all. The kitchen became a battleground, with kale smoothies, thanks to the detailed recipes from Gouhrravv over their years of friendship, and cabbage soups standing guard against the looming XL tag.

Meera, concerned for her friend, attempted an intervention. "Aarya, you're beautiful just the way you are. This wedding is about celebrating love, not losing weight."

But Aarya, fuelled by the pressure to fit into her imagined M-sized glory, wouldn't be swayed. "Meera, I need to do this for myself. I want to walk into that wedding feeling like a goddess, not a statistic on an XL tag."

Days turned into a hilarious saga of Aarya's weight-loss exploits. CrossFit tutorials were attempted, green teas were consumed by the gallon, and Aarya's Fitbit became her sworn ally. The pressure cooker saw more action than ever before, as Aarya dabbled in culinary experiments that could rival a Michelin-starred diet plan.

She also met a self-proclaimed expert nutritionist from her building who had specially curated weight loss diet plans. Consider the "Cucumber Symphony Diet," where every meal involves serenading your taste buds with the monotony of cucumber-centric creations. From cucumber smoothies to cucumber pasta (yes, that's a thing), this diet claims to peel away pounds faster than you can say, "Is there life beyond cucumbers?"

And let's not overlook the "Kaleidoscopic Cleanse," where your world turns into a vibrant kaleidoscope of green. Kale, kale, and more kale – breakfast, lunch, dinner, and kale-flavoured snacks in between. Because who needs variety when you can have all shades of green, right?

"Or perhaps you've heard of the "Breatharian Ballet," an avant-garde performance that insists you can subsist on air alone. Forget food; just breathe in deeply, and voilà, you're on the path to enlightenment and maybe a touch of dizziness", Meera joked.

Caught between laughter and concern, Meera witnessed Aarya's transformation from an office whiz to a weight-loss warrior. "Aarya, you're turning into a fitness influencer's nightmare. Let's find a middle ground, okay?"

But Aarya, fuelled by the wedding countdown, remained undeterred. The wedding weight-off was on, and the XL tag was her ultimate nemesis.

As the days dwindled down to the grand celebration, Aarya's metamorphosis became the talk of her social circle. Friends marvelled at her dedication, and the local vegetable vendor started stocking up on kale and lemons, courtesy of Aarya's newfound obsessions.

The countdown to the wedding turned into a comedy of errors, with Aarya's Fitbit logging more steps than a marathon and her kitchen resembling a science lab of bizarre concoctions. Meera, forever the supportive friend, tried her best to keep the mood light amidst the chaos.

The grand three-day wedding loomed on the horizon, and Aarya, armed with a newfound determination, was ready to face the festivities with the triumphant aura of one who had conquered the XL challenge.

CHAPTER 12

Desserts, Decisions, and Digital Dalliances

The three-day wedding bonanza had finally arrived, and Aarya found herself standing in front of her wardrobe like a general surveying her troops. She had scoured the malls with Meera, engaged in a tumultuous weight-off, and now, clad in a saree that rivalled the night sky, she was ready to face Aashish's grand celebration.

As she admired her reflection, a slight pang of sadness crept in. Meera, her partner-in-crime, was nowhere to be seen. The influencer-con had claimed Meera for the first two days, leaving Aarya to navigate the wedding battlefield solo until the final day. Betrayal was a harsh word, but Aarya couldn't help feeling a bit abandoned.

Just as she was contemplating Meera's absence, her phone pinged with an incoming email. Aarya raised an eyebrow as she saw the sender's name – Pratik, the annoying Gen-Z assistant she had hired recently to have a younger audience POV for her podcast. She quickly put her phone away while getting into the car to head to the venue. The email notification kept blinking in her phone.

The subject line read: "URGENT: Work Woes and Weekend Whimsy."

Aarya sighed and opened the email, bracing herself for a barrage of emojis and acronyms. The email read:

Hey Aarya,

Hope this email finds you vibin' and thrivin' and slayin' the wedding game. Just wanted to slide into your inbox (virtual high-five for keeping it clutter-free, by the way) with a quick work sitch that's been giving us some major FOMO.

So, here's the 411: our project is low-key slaying, but it's been getting a bit extra, and we're not sure if it's boujee or just doing the absolute most. Can we circle back during our next virtual pow-wow to spill the tea and figure out if we're flexing too hard or if it's just the universe throwing some shade?

Also, low-key obsessed with that idea you dropped in the last meeting – total game-changer! Can we get a moment to brainstorm together and see if we can turn it into something Insta-worthy? I've got some killer snackables ready for our brainstorm sesh – the virtual fridge is stocked!

Let me know when you're free, and we can sync up to untangle this web of adulting. Catch you on the flip side!

Best,

Prat.

Aarya blinked at the screen, trying to decipher the cryptic message. "Gen-Z hieroglyphics," she muttered under her breath.

Amidst the kaleidoscope of colours and the rhythmic beats of the wedding festivities, Aarya found herself standing at the entrance of the grand venue, adorned in her carefully chosen wedding guest ensemble. Just as she was taking in the opulence around her, Aashish, the groom himself, emerged from the lively crowd with a beaming smile that rivalled the splendour of the occasion.

"Aarya! It's been too long," Aashish exclaimed, pulling her into a warm hug. "I'm so glad you could make it. Meet my beautiful bride, Isha." Aarya turned to see Isha, radiant in her bridal attire, standing beside Aashish. Isha's eyes sparkled with joy, and the warmth of her greeting made Aarya feel like an old friend rather than a kind-of ex. "Aarya, I've heard so much about you. Aashish talks about you all the time," Isha said with genuine enthusiasm. Aarya, caught in the whirlwind of grandeur and genuine hospitality, exchanged pleasantries with the newlyweds, silently relieved that the awkwardness she anticipated had melted away in the embrace of their welcoming smiles.

Just as she was about to breathe a sigh of relief, a familiar voice cut through the air – Latha aunty and her platoon were on the horizon.

"Ah, Aarya! You're looking absolutely stunning," Latha aunty exclaimed, her eyes scanning Aarya from head to toe. "Come, join us. We're heading to the dessert counter. The Gulab Jamuns are calling your name!"

Aarya forced a smile and fell into step with the Latha platoon. As they descended upon the dessert table like a swarm of fashion-forward locusts, the air filled with whispers and hushed gossip. Aarya was now the center of attention, and Latha aunty made sure everyone knew it.

The drama continued as the platoon dissected every aspect of Aarya's life – her career, her relationship status (or lack thereof), and, of course, the grand wedding. Aarya, trapped in this vortex of scrutiny, longed for an escape.

Just when she thought the ordeal was over, Latha aunty handed her the ultimate responsibility – babysitting two hyperactive siblings who seemed to have harnessed the energy of a thousand suns. Aarya, now tasked with preventing a toddler tornado, found herself regretting every life choice that led her to this moment.

Desperate times called for desperate measures, and Aarya resorted to playing a video of Coco Melon on her phone, hoping to lull the little ones into a temporary trance. As she navigated the treacherous waters of nursery rhymes, an ad popped up on her feed – a beacon of hope in the chaos.

"Bumble – Find Your Perfect Match!"

Aarya blinked, her mind racing with possibilities. Was this a sign from the universe amidst the kiddie cacophony? She contemplated the idea for a moment, imagining a life where her assistant's emails were the least of her concerns.

The wedding whirlwind continued around her – the platoon still gossiping, the kids now distracted by the wonders of digital entertainment, and Aarya lost in a sea of contemplation.

As the night wore on, and the wedding festivities reached their crescendo, Aarya found herself standing at the crossroads of responsibility and rebellion. Bumble was calling her, and so was the siren song of a dance floor that beckoned with promises of freedom.

To swipe or not to swipe, that was the question.

Chapter 13

SWIPES AND SERENDIPITY

Aarya found herself caught in the crossfire of decisions – to swipe or not to swipe. The dance floor pulsed with energy, the rhythm of Bollywood numbers vibrating through the air as Aashish and Isha made their grand entrance, a vision straight out of a Yash Raj film. Aarya, standing on the side-lines, watched the spectacle unfold with a mixture of awe and cynicism.

As Aashish twirled Isha amidst the entourage of perfectly choreographed dancers, the whispers of the background crowd reached Aarya's ears. "50 crores dowry, a Mercedes Benz, and the snack empire – talk about a jackpot," someone murmured. Aarya couldn't help but let out a sarcastic grin, the absurdity of the situation not lost on her.

Determined to escape the melodramatic spectacle, Aarya decided it was time to delve into the chaotic world of online dating. With a swipe, she embarked on a journey that promised a mix of cringe-worthy questionnaires and the faint hope of stumbling upon someone who could tolerate her quirks.

The never-ending questionnaire began – age, interests, favourite ice cream flavour (as if that was a personality trait). Aarya navigated through the maze of checkboxes and text boxes, her eyes rolling at the sheer predictability of it all. Just when she thought she might succumb to a carpal tunnel from excessive scrolling, it was finally time to swipe.

She hesitated for a moment, her thumb hovering over the screen. What did she really want? The grandeur of Aashish's wedding served as a stark reminder of the societal expectations she couldn't escape. But perhaps, amidst the sea of profiles, a silver lining awaited.

She swiped through a few profiles, each one more lacklustre than the last. Aarya's skepticism grew with every passing photo, and the first three matches didn't even last as long as it took to make Maggi noodles. She was on the verge of giving up on the virtual quest for love when a new interest notification appeared.

Aarya's eyes focused on the screen, scanning the profile with a cautious optimism. The profile picture featured a guy holding a guitar, his bio mentioned a love for spontaneous road trips and a fondness for cheesy jokes. Aarya found herself intrigued – a refreshing change from the generic profiles she had encountered thus far.

With a deep breath, she swiped right.

It was a match.

Aarya couldn't help but feel a twinge of excitement. Was this the beginning of a new love story, or just another fleeting digital connection? The notifications chimed, signalling a potential conversation awaiting her attention.

The chat window opened, and Aarya found herself face-to-face (or rather, text-to-text) with someone who seemed refreshingly unpretentious.

DhruvSays: Hey there! ⊠ Just swiped right because I've got a feeling we could out-sass each other in cheesy jokes. What's your go-to road trip snack?

Aarya chuckled at the message, appreciating the humour that seemed genuine. She replied:

AaryaVibes: Hey! ⊠ Road trips are my jam. Nachos and a solid playlist are non-negotiable. What about you? Any snack preferences or just down for a culinary adventure?

And so began the banter – a volley of messages exchanged between two strangers navigating the unpredictable terrain of online conversations. They shared stories of favourite road trip memories, debated the superiority of waffles versus pancakes, and unearthed a shared love for obscure '90s sitcoms.

DhruvSays: So, what's the weirdest thing about you that you'd put in an online dating bio?

AaryaVibes: Oh, you know, just the usual – I can recite the entire dialogue of 'Friends' and make a killer avocado toast. What about you?

DhruvSays: I have a collection of rubber ducks. Each one has a name and a backstory. Don't judge.

AaryaVibes: Not judging, just impressed. The weirder, the better!

As the messages flowed, Aarya couldn't help but feel a spark of intrigue. Perhaps amidst the chaos of wedding drama and societal expectations, she had stumbled upon an unexpected connection. The virtual realm of swipes and chats, though fraught with uncertainties, held the potential for something genuinely serendipitous.

CHAPTER 14

CHATS AND CHEERS

The virtual banter between Aarya and Dhruv continued, each message weaving a tapestry of shared jokes, quirky preferences, and the promise of potential connection. Aarya, excited about the unexpected turn of events, decided to share the news with her confidantes – Meera and Gouhrravv.

Opening her group chat, Aarya typed with a sense of anticipation:

AaryaVibes: Hey, you two! Guess what? Remember that Bumble match I mentioned? Well, it turns out we've been having some pretty awesome conversations.

Meera and Gouhrravv responded almost simultaneously:

MeeraMagic: No way! spill the chai, Aarya. Give us the deets!

GouhrravvWokeness: spill it, queen! spill it like your favourite avocado toast.

AaryaVibes: Haha, you two! Alright, so, his name is Dhruv, and he's got this adorable collection of rubber ducks. We've been talking about everything – road trips,

'90s sitcoms, and even the weird things we'd put in our online dating bios. It's surprisingly fun!

MeeraMagic: That sounds like the start of a rom-com! I'm so happy for you, Aarya. Maybe this is your chance at romance, and you won't have to dive into the arranged marriage circus.

GouhrravvWokeness: Yasss, Aarya! Romance vibes all the way. Forget the business contract weddings, and let love do its thing.

AaryaVibes: Thanks, you two! It does feel different this time. And guess what? Meera, you'll be here tomorrow, right? Kriya is bringing her partner, Shipra, tomorrow. I've heard so much about her, and I'm excited to meet her finally.

MeeraMagic: That's fantastic news! Our little group is growing. Let the good vibes roll!

AaryaVibes: We will miss you G! But we will keep you posted!!

As the group chat buzzed with excitement, Aarya continued her conversations with Dhruv. Amidst the laughter and shared anecdotes, a surprising revelation surfaced – Dhruv was coming to Aarya's town the next day to visit his aunt.

AaryaVibes: Hold up, Dhruv! You're coming to town tomorrow?

DhruvSays: Yeah, my aunt lives there. Small world, huh?

AaryaVibes: Small, indeed! Well, maybe we can grab a coffee or something. What do you think?

DhruvSays: I'd love that! Consider it a date.

Aarya couldn't help but feel a mix of excitement and nerves. A coffee date with someone she met on Bumble – it was uncharted territory, a departure from the familiarity of her usual routine.

Ah, the illustrious Indian arranged marriage system – a well-choreographed ballet of tradition and societal expectations, where your love life is less a romantic comedy and more a suspense thriller with too many plot twists. It all starts with the cosmic compatibility check, where the stars decide if you and your potential partner are a celestial match made in heaven or if your zodiac signs need couples therapy.

Enter the resume scrutiny phase – because who needs dating apps when you have family members armed with a checklist that can rival a NASA mission brief? Your qualifications, career aspirations, and the number of times you've blinked since birth are up for inspection. Forget about personal preferences; we're talking about lineage, financial stability, and the brand of toothpaste you use.

Then comes the 'rishta' meeting, the real-life version of a job interview where you're both the candidate and the position. The awkward small talk flows like a leaky tap, and genuine connection takes a backseat to more pressing matters like whether you can carry a conversation with the neighbour's cat.

The grand finale – the wedding – is a dazzling spectacle where your personal desires are gently nudged backstage, and family expectations take the spotlight. As you exchange garlands and sacred vows, it's as if you're the protagonist in a play directed by your great aunt twice removed.

But fear not, for within this circus of cultural expectations, love does occasionally rear its head. It's the surprise ending in a movie you thought you had figured out, a glimmer of spontaneity in a sea of pre-determined steps. It's like trying to find a needle in a haystack but stumbling upon a diamond instead.

So, as the generations continue this dance of arranged marriages, we cling to the hope that amidst the checklist evaluations and celestial negotiations, true connections will emerge – because, after all, love has a knack for playing hide-and-seek even in the most unlikely of places.

As for now, the prospect of a potential connection loomed on the horizon, and Aarya found herself wondering if this encounter could evolve into something beyond the virtual realm. As the night unfolded, Aarya couldn't shake off the feeling of anticipation. Dhruv's impending visit, Meera's arrival, and the prospect of meeting Shipra and Kriya added layers of excitement to the air. The group chat continued to buzz with messages of cheer, turning the virtual space into a haven of positivity and camaraderie.

CHAPTER 15

THE BIG DAY

The day unfolded with Aarya's breezy response to Pratik's email, a stark contrast to the high-energetic "Gen-z lingo" tone he had set. It was a signal, a simple "Sure, let's do tomorrow at 2 pm," that hinted at a newfound clarity in Aarya's mind. With a grin that had been absent for a while, she approached the day with a lightness of spirit.

Today marked the grand wedding celebration of Aashish, and surprisingly, Aarya was feeling remarkably chill about it. Donning a breath-taking lehenga, she was ready to revel in the love and festivities, her friends by her side.

Kriya and Shipra, the epitome of a Bollywood couple, welcomed Aarya into the venue. Shipra's infectious energy made her an instant favourite, and Aarya mentally applauded Kriya for her excellent taste in life partners. Then, in a delightful twist, Meera strutted in with her plus one – none other than the woke buddy himself, Gouhrravv. They had apparently been working on a little love project of their own and wanted to surprise Aarya. Aarya couldn't be more thrilled. The whimsical duo was transitioning from dream to reality.

For Aarya, stepping into Aashish and Isha's wedding venue felt like being whisked away to a magical realm. The enchanting setting was embraced by nature, surrounded by verdant greenery and adorned with an explosion of vibrant flowers, creating an ambiance straight out of a fairy tale. As they strolled down the pathway, lit by the soft glow of twinkling lights on towering trees, the air carried the sweet fragrance of blossoms, immersing her in a dreamy atmosphere.

The focal point of the celebration, the grand courtyard, stood as a testament to romance and opulence. With majestic marble columns standing tall, it transformed into a canvas of floral wonders. Delicate vines of jasmine and ivy cascaded from above, framing the stage where Aashish and Isha would exchange their vows. The stage itself was a regal spectacle, draped in opulent fabric and adorned with golden accents, echoing the grandeur of their love.

Seated on elegant Chiavari chairs, they marvelled at the tables adorned with luxurious fabrics in hues of ivory, blush, and gold. Each table hosted an artful center piece, while crystal chandeliers overhead cast a soft, romantic glow, enhancing the overall enchantment of the scene.

The water feature, a winding stream adorned with floating candles and delicate petals, added a touch of serenity to the festivities. The gentle trickle of water became a soothing melody, creating a serene oasis amidst the celebratory buzz.

Exploring the venue further, Aarya discovered themed alcoves, each narrating a chapter of Aashish and Isha's love story through photographs and creative installations. It was like walking through a gallery of cherished memories, a testament to the beautiful journey they had undertaken together.

As the sun dipped below the horizon, the venue underwent a magical transformation. Fairy lights adorned the trees, casting a sparkling glow, and lanterns guided the way, turning the surroundings into a celestial garden beneath the moonlit sky.

The wedding venue, with its whimsical charm, became more than just a location; it embodied the celebration of love. Every detail, from the intricate decorations to the soft illumination, painted a portrait of dreams intertwined with reality. It was a place where emotions soared, leaving an indelible mark on everyone's heart as they witnessed the grandeur of Aashish and Isha's love story.

Amidst laughter, delicious food, and the warm camaraderie of friends, Aashish and Isha were gearing up for their pheras. However, Aarya found herself inadvertently in the line of fire, surrounded by the aunties and Latha aunty leading the charge. Latha aunty, with a sly smile, decided to play the matchmaking maestro, saying, "Aarya, if only you had moved a little faster, you could have been the one wearing the bridal lehenga today." The comment, a classic blend of societal expectations and traditional matchmaking tactics, struck a nerve. Aarya, fuelled by years of pent-up frustration, unleashed a tirade of words in direct response to Latha aunty's matchmaking manoeuvres.

"Well, Latha aunty, I'm quite content being a solo act in this circus of life," Aarya retorted with a wry smile. "Marriage isn't a race, and I'm not competing for the 'Spinster of the Year' award. I'll marry for love, not for societal checkboxes and dowry negotiations. And as for my biological clock, I can always freeze my eggs or even adopt. Besides, I've got a front-row seat to the wedding spectacle, and that's entertainment enough for me!"

The venue fell into stunned silence. The bride and groom, guests, and even the catering staff stared at Aarya in shock. It wasn't exactly the speech one expected at a wedding, but the words had a life of their own.

Meera, the eternal rock of support, gently pulled Aarya away from the auntie ambush, reminding her that Latha aunty had provoked the verbal explosion. As Aarya collected herself, she couldn't shake off the lingering embarrassment. The wedding concluded, leaving Aarya half-dead but cheered on by her friends.

Later, a message from Dhruv interrupted her post-wedding reflections. He was waiting at the coffee shop with a surprise. Aarya, ready for a delightful diversion, eagerly prepared to meet him.

As she stepped into the coffee shop, the aura of embarrassment from the wedding antics lingered, but Aarya was determined to leave it behind. The coffee shop exuded a cozy charm, the aroma of freshly brewed coffee wafting through the air. Dhruv sat at a corner table, a warm smile playing on his lips as he noticed Aarya approaching. He rose to greet her, and the genuine excitement in his eyes hinted at a surprise that piqued her curiosity.

As they settled into our seats, the atmosphere was comfortable and easy going. Dhruv's presence was calming, and his conversation flowed effortlessly, creating an engaging connection. He had a way of making you feel heard, a quality that stood out like a beacon in a world full of distractions.

Dhruv, with a smile that hinted at a surprise, ushered in the unexpected twist – his aunt was there to meet Aarya. Aarya was a little stunned at the sudden "Meeting the family" action that was happening, but she remained positive. He seemed like the Mr. Right after all. She prepared herself to say hello when she turned around to see none other than Latha aunty. It was the same Latha aunty that had received the brunt of Aarya's wrath earlier that day. Dhruv was her nephew and it was indeed an unexpected turn of events.

Aarya's internal scream of "Noooooooo" reverberated through the coffee shop, turning what could have been a romantic meeting into a cringe-worthy sitcom moment.

Part 2

THE NEPHEW CONUNDRUM

The reality hit Aarya like a freight train—Dhruv, the charming Bumble match, was Latha aunty's nephew. The awkward smile etched on Aarya's face mirrored the shock reflected on Latha aunty's features. It was a spectacle frozen in time, a moment captured straight out of a cringe-worthy sitcom.

Seemingly oblivious to the tension, Dhruv kept the conversation flowing. "Aunty, Aarya is absolutely amazing. Such a brilliant mind, and her sense of humour is unparalleled," Dhruv praised, and Aarya couldn't help but cringe internally. The residual effects of the verbal tsunami she had unleashed at the wedding were still echoing in her mind.

Latha aunty, recovering from the initial shock, seized the opportunity to paint a picture of Dhruv as the perfect catch. "Oh yes, Dhruv is the jewel of our family, a rising star in his field. Aarya, you're truly lucky to have matched with him."

Aarya managed a tight-lipped smile, the unease settling deeper. Dhruv, taking the lead in the conversation, began narrating tales of his achievements, hobbies, and future plans. Each word felt like a reminder of the storm that awaited Aarya.

As the conversation continued, Aarya found herself trapped in a web of polite nods and forced smiles. Dhruv, seemingly charmed by the potential of this love connection, went on praising his family, values, and the close-knit bond they shared.

Deep inside, Aarya couldn't shake off the feeling that she had unwittingly stepped into a trap of her own making. The more Dhruv spoke, the more she realized the depth of her verbal blunder at the wedding. She couldn't help but wonder if Latha aunty, with a masterstroke of matchmaking finesse, had orchestrated this meeting, and Aarya was at the center of it all.

While Dhruv painted a glowing picture of Aarya to his aunty and vice versa, the two women sat there awkwardly nodding, still shaken to the core. The wedding fiasco had morphed into a tangled mess, and Aarya wondered if there was an exit strategy from this uncomfortable rendezvous.

Aarya, desperate to escape the labyrinth of familial matchmaking, seized the first opportunity to excuse herself from the seemingly orchestrated encounter. She mumbled something about needing to check on a friend and practically sprinted away from the Latha aunty-Dhruv alliance. Once at a safe distance, she frantically dialled Meera's number, eager to share the absurdity of the situation.

Meera, blissfully immersed in her new kale smoothie routine with Gouhrravv, answered the call. Aarya spilled the beans about the awkward tête-à-tête, leaving Meera momentarily silent. Then, in a fit of disbelief, Meera nearly spat out her green concoction.

"Wait, wait, wait! You're telling me that Latha aunty's nephew is the same Dhruv from Bumble? The universe is playing an epic prank on you, Aarya," Meera exclaimed, wiping kale smoothie off her chin.

Aarya, still recovering from the shock, couldn't shake off the suspicion that this might indeed be Latha aunty's handiwork. Meera, however, urged her friend to give her the benefit of the doubt. "Latha aunty orchestrating a Bumble connection? That's a little too much, even for her. Maybe it's just a cosmic coincidence. Let's not jump to conclusions just yet," Meera advised, offering a shred of optimism amidst the chaos of kale-infused revelations.

CHAPTER 2

THE AFTERMATH

Aarya's phone buzzed with Dhruv's messages, each one reflecting his growing concern. She glanced at the screen, contemplating how to respond. In a moment of exhaustion and exasperation, she texted back, "Hey, it's been a long day. Can we catch up tomorrow? Good night." She hesitated for a moment before reluctantly hitting send.

Dhruv, interpreting her message as a sign of distress, sent a flurry of cheesy good night texts, each one inducing a cringe in Aarya's stomach. She decided to mute her phone and bury herself under the covers, hoping to escape the surreal events of the day. "Maybe it's just a weird dream, and tomorrow I'll wake up with everything back to normal," she thought, closing her eyes and drifting into an uneasy sleep.

The next morning arrived with the promise of a fresh start, but Aarya's hopes were quickly dashed. As she stumbled into the kitchen, her mother greeted her with a warm smile and some sandwiches. However, the air thickened with anticipation as Aarya's mother declared, "Family meeting after breakfast. I have something important to discuss."

Aarya's heart sank. Her mother had gotten a whiff of what unravelled at the wedding, probably from the town newspaper (it was a small town and a grand wedding, after all) or from her mother's most reliable source, a WhatsApp group of the colony aunties, possibly with pictures and videos. Ah! The beauty of technology! Aarya knew what was coming - The timeless lecture on the virtues of a 'good girl' from a 'good family.' Her mother believed that maintaining a soft-spoken, respectful demeanour was the key to securing Prince Charming and riding off into marital bliss. Aarya couldn't help but roll her eyes at the antiquated notions that still persisted.

As they gathered around the table, Aarya's mother began her monologue, seamlessly transitioning from one cliché to another. Aarya fought the urge to tune out as her mother passionately outlined the societal expectations that burdened young women. She sighed, wondering how long it would take for her mother to realize that Aarya's pursuit of happiness didn't align with these age-old stereotypes.

Midway through the lecture, Aarya's phone pinged, a timely interruption to the verbose discourse. She discreetly checked the message – a reminder from Pratik about their 2 pm meeting. Coffee was urgently required to navigate through the sea of clichés and misplaced concerns.

Aarya excused herself, promising to return shortly, and retreated to her sanctuary – the coffee maker. As the aromatic brew filled the kitchen, she took a moment to gather her thoughts. The impending meeting with

Pratik was a welcome distraction from the familial storm brewing around her.

With a steaming mug in hand, Aarya settled into her makeshift home office, ready to face whatever work challenges awaited her.

As Aarya joined her Zoom call, she was greeted by the ever-enthusiastic Pratik, her Gen-Z assistant with a flair for digital communication. With a casual "Sup, Aarya?" he dived right into the conversation, seamlessly blending work queries with colloquial charm.

"Yo, how's the wedding scene back in your hometown? Any drama or is it all just vibes?" Pratik inquired, his virtual background subtly flashing neon signs of a party scene. Aarya chuckled, sharing snippets of the three-day wedding bonanza.

Then came the big reveal – Pratik had exciting plans lincd up for Aarya. "Guess what? I've got some guests lined up for your podcast! We're talking industry experts, influencers, and maybe a surprise or two. Your show's gonna be lit!"

Aarya, both excited and apprehensive, expressed her concerns about landing big names for her novice podcast. "I mean, I'm just starting out, Pratik. Will they even consider being on my show?"

With an air of confidence that defined his generation, Pratik responded, "Trust me, Aarya, it's all about networking, marketing, and communication. Leave it to me; we'll have your podcast buzzing in no time. Just focus on bringing your A-game during the interviews, and we'll handle the rest."

Amidst the podcast plans, Pratik slipped in another question, "By the way, when are you heading back to your abode from the hometown fiesta? We've got some prep to do, and I need my podcast maestro back in action!"

CHAPTER 3

BREWING LATTE, BREWING ROMANCE

The wedding saga had finally concluded, and Aarya, Meera, and Gouhrravv found themselves back in the comforting embrace of their own world. The echoes of wedding vows and dance beats were replaced by the familiar humdrum of daily life.

Determined to shake off the wedding drama, Aarya decided to plunge headfirst into work. As she sat at her desk, she took a decisive step – the deletion of her Bumble profile. The app was swiftly uninstalled, and Aarya thought she had successfully put the unexpected rendezvous with Dhruv behind her.

However, the digital remnants of their interaction lingered. Dhruv's messages continued to punctuate her phone screen, waiting for a response that seemed elusive. Meera's voice echoed in her mind, suggesting that maybe it was all just a bizarre coincidence orchestrated by the universe.

Unable to dismiss the feeling of responsibility, Aarya contemplated her next move. She couldn't leave Dhruv hanging, oblivious to the quirky events that transpired at the wedding. So, with a sigh, she picked up her phone and dialled his number.

"Hey Dhruv," Aarya began, her voice a blend of apprehension and determination. "How about we meet up? There's this cozy café I've been meaning to check out. Tomorrow at 4 pm?"

Dhruv, on the other end of the line, seemed pleasantly surprised by the proposition. "Sure, Aarya! I'd love that. Which café are we talking about?"

As Aarya shared the details, she couldn't help but wonder how this impromptu meeting would unfold. Little did she know that the cozy café setting was about to become the backdrop for the next chapter in her unexpected rendezvous with the universe. The latte art on her coffee might just mirror the intricate dance of possibilities that awaited her.

∗ ∗ ∗

The café buzzed with the hum of quiet conversations and the hiss of the espresso machine. Aarya and Dhruv sat across from each other, the awkwardness palpable as they navigated the aftermath of a wedding fiasco and the unspoken tension that lingered between them. A tentative smile played on Aarya's lips as she sipped her coffee, attempting to break the ice that had formed around them.

Before Aarya could voice her apologies for the radio silence, Dhruv interjected with a reassuring tone, "Aarya, there's no need to apologize. If anyone should be sorry, it's me." His sincerity caught Aarya off guard, and she furrowed her brows in confusion.

"I had no idea about what happened at the wedding until Latha aunty filled me in yesterday," Dhruv continued, his expression turning apologetic. "I'm genuinely sorry about that, and I want you to know that I support you. Latha aunty's comments were out of line, and your response was completely reasonable."

Aarya's eyes widened in surprise. She hadn't expected this turn of events. Dhruv wasn't part of some orchestrated plan; he genuinely seemed oblivious to the chaos that had ensued at the wedding. A wave of relief washed over her as she realized that maybe, just maybe, Dhruv wasn't another pawn in Latha aunty's matchmaking game.

As Dhruv expressed his disappointment in his aunt's actions, Aarya couldn't help but feel a growing sense of admiration for him. Perhaps he wasn't cut from the same cloth as Latha aunty. The weight of uncertainty lifted from Aarya's shoulders, replaced by a newfound ease in Dhruv's company.

With a sigh of relief and a genuine smile, Aarya resumed sipping her coffee. The tension that had hung in the air began to dissipate, paving the way for a more relaxed conversation. But just as Aarya thought they were settling into a comfortable rhythm, Dhruv threw in an unexpected twist.

In a move that left the café staff and patrons equally surprised, Dhruv dropped to one knee, his eyes locking onto Aarya's. "Aarya," he declared, "I don't want to let this connection between us slip away. Will you marry me?"

Aarya's heart skipped a beat. She felt a flush of embarrassment rise to her cheeks. The café, once a haven of quiet conversations, now held its breath as all eyes turned to the unexpected proposal. Caught off guard and unable to process the surreal turn of events, Aarya sat there, speechless and motionless, grappling with the unexpected proposition that hung in the air.

CHAPTER 4

THE PROPOSAL

Aarya sat frozen in her chair, the warmth of the latte turning into a peculiar mix of surprise and bewilderment. Her initial agenda for the meeting was crystal clear – to sever any budding connection between her and Dhruv. But here he was, on bended knee, asking a question that seemed to echo through the hushed café.

Dhruv's eyes sparkled with sincerity, awaiting her response. Aarya, still grappling with the shock, tried to piece together a coherent thought. She looked around, half-expecting hidden cameras to reveal a prank, but the surrounding patrons were oblivious to the mini-drama unfolding.

"I... I don't understand," Aarya stammered, her eyes darting from Dhruv to the ring he held in his hand. The café staff had paused in their duties, curiosity evident in their eyes.

Dhruv, undeterred by the public setting, spoke with earnest conviction. "Aarya, from the moment we started talking, I felt a connection, something rare and special. I don't want to let that slip away. I want you to be a part of my life in a way that goes beyond just chats and casual meetings."

Aarya, still in a state of shock, managed to whisper, "But... we've only met twice, and the first time was under such bizarre circumstances. Are you sure about this?"

Dhruv's smile remained unwavering. "Sometimes, life throws surprises our way, and we just need to go with the flow. I can't explain it, but I feel a strong connection with you. Let's navigate this journey together, and who knows what wonders it might bring."

Aarya, her mind a whirlwind of conflicting thoughts, looked down at Dhruv's earnest face. The café seemed to hold its breath, awaiting her response. In that moment of uncertainty, Aarya pondered the possibility of this unexpected twist in her life's narrative. The latte sat forgotten, the warmth replaced by a cascade of emotions that left her torn between caution and curiosity.

* * *

The seconds stretched into an agonizing silence as Aarya grappled with the unexpected proposal and the eyes of the café patrons bore into her. Murmurs rippled through the air, and sympathetic glances were exchanged as people began to feel sorry for Dhruv, who still knelt on one knee, his hopeful gaze fixed on Aarya.

"Aarya!" Dhruv's voice broke through the hush, cutting sharply against the tense atmosphere. "What do you say? Will you be my forever?"

The pressure in the room intensified. Aarya felt the weight of everyone's expectations pressing down on her, and she knew she had to respond. The chant of "say yes" echoed around her, urging her to make a decision, any decision, to break the heavy silence.

Taking a deep breath, Aarya hesitated for a moment longer, feeling the weight of the moment on her shoulders. The anticipation in Dhruv's eyes was palpable. The café patrons held their collective breath, waiting for the verdict.

Finally, unable to withstand the pressure and wanting to end the suspense, Aarya uttered a hesitant but audible, "Yes." The word hung in the air, breaking the silence and setting off a wave of applause from the onlookers. Dhruv's face lit up with joy as he stood up, and the café erupted into a mixture of cheers and congratulations.

Aarya, on the other hand, felt a turmoil of emotions. She couldn't believe she had just agreed to marry someone she had met briefly, especially after the chaos at the wedding. The reality of the situation sank in, and she wondered what she had gotten herself into. As the applause continued, Aarya's mind raced with a million thoughts, but amidst the cacophony of emotions, the one thing that echoed loud and clear was the undeniable fact that her life had taken an unexpected turn, and there was no turning back.

CHAPTER 5

VIRTUAL STORM

Aarya reluctantly dragged herself off the couch, her tangled hair and the remnants of yesterday's mascara giving her a dishevelled appearance. After yesterday's eventful adventure, Aarya retreated to the comforting embrace of her couch, a bucket of ice cream in hand, ready to embark on a marathon of her favourite sitcoms. The doorbell's persistent ring echoed in her ears as she stumbled toward it. Vanitha Didi, her house help, with her usual stern expression, unleashed a cascade of complaints about the state of Aarya's apartment.

"Are you planning to open a restaurant under the sofa, madam? And why is your phone off? I have tried ringing it non-stop. Have you heard of Gupta Ji's affair with that new lady from the second floor?" Vanitha Didi's lecture accompanied Aarya's attempts to salvage some semblance of order from the chaos.

With Vanitha Didi's critiques fading into the background, Aarya retreated to the comforting embrace of her couch. She sighed, realizing that even in her own space, she couldn't escape the demands of the world.

As she contemplated the surreal turn of events, Aarya decided it was time to face the digital realm. She hesitantly powered up her phone, and as it came to life, the incessant notifications bombarded her senses.

WhatsApp messages overflowed, each containing a mix of congratulatory wishes, curious inquiries, and well-meaning advice. Aarya's Facebook page, once a serene oasis, had transformed into a virtual battleground. Dhruv's engagement post was flooded with reactions, comments, and shares.

Meera's call interrupted Aarya's silent contemplation. She hesitated before answering, unsure of how to navigate the verbal whirlwind that awaited her. "Aarya, are you okay?" Meera's concern echoed through the phone.

Aarya managed a feeble, "I'm not sure," as she listened to Meera's empathetic words. The virtual storm had taken over her life, and the eye of the hurricane was nowhere in sight.

Meera, being the voice of reason, suggested that Aarya address the situation head-on. "You can't avoid this, Aarya. We need a strategy to handle the aftermath. And remember, I'm here for you, every step of the way."

With a deep breath, Aarya braced herself for the inevitable. She knew that shutting herself off wasn't a sustainable solution. The virtual storm had swept her into unmapped territories, and she had to find a way to navigate through the chaos.

Aarya plunged back into her work, attempting to find solace in the familiar rhythm of her professional life. Amidst the sea of notifications, Pratik's congratulatory message on her recent engagement stood out like a digital beacon. She responded with a courteous "Thanks," though the weight of her recent whirlwind proposal still lingered in the periphery.

Driven by a mix of curiosity and a need for distraction, Aarya redirected the conversation toward Pratik's grand podcast plans. Much to her surprise, Pratik animatedly revealed that he had pulled off a significant coup – securing a podcast session with none other than "KABIR SINGHANIYA." The name echoed through the digital space, and Aarya's eyes widened with a blend of disbelief and excitement.

Kabir Singhania, a formidable Indian entrepreneur, had recently earned a coveted spot in the prestigious "40 under 40" list by BIZ WORLD, the preeminent digital business magazine that delved into the cutting-edge realms of artificial intelligence, innovation, and the Internet of Things. As Aarya absorbed the magnitude of this revelation, a surge of enthusiasm replaced the cloud of personal turmoil that hung over her.

Despite the chaos that had become her personal life, the prospect of hosting Kabir Singhania on her podcast injected a renewed sense of purpose. The nerves were undeniable, but the allure of engaging in a conversation with a business luminary trumped any reservations. As she prepared to navigate discussions on innovation and entrepreneurship, Aarya found a silver lining amid the turbulence. The podcast session emerged as a beacon of positivity, offering a welcome escape from the tumult that had engulfed her reality.

As Aarya basked in the exhilaration of the upcoming podcast session with Kabir Singhania, her phone interrupted the momentary bliss. A familiar ringtone signalled an incoming call, and when she glanced at the screen, a wave of disbelief washed over her. It was her mother. The timing couldn't have been worse, or so she thought.

Answering the call with a mix of anticipation and trepidation, Aarya's mother greeted her with the usual warmth, but there was an underlying gravity to her tone. "Aarya, beta, your father and I are planning to visit you in town. We have some important matters to discuss with Dhruv's parents. It's about time our families meet and discuss the upcoming union."

Aarya's excitement plummeted to the depths of apprehension. The realization hit her like a sudden gust of wind – the engagement that seemed like a surreal nightmare was now turning into a tangible reality. She stammered out a response, attempting to feign enthusiasm while her mind raced to comprehend the tornado of events. Meeting Dhruv's parents was a significant leap into a future she had not anticipated, and the weight of this revelation hung heavy in the air.

As she disconnected the call, Aarya grappled with conflicting emotions. The juxtaposition of professional highs and personal challenges created a complex tapestry of emotions. The impending visit marked a juncture where her carefully crafted worlds collided, and she couldn't help but wonder how the threads of her life would weave together in the days to come.

SAMOSAS AND SUBTLE SUSPICIONS

As Aarya sat in her modest apartment, surrounded by the awkwardness that hung in the air like a dense fog, she couldn't help but question the series of events that had led her to this peculiar juncture. The saree she wore felt like an uncomfortable costume, a stark reminder of the traditional dance she found herself entangled in.

Dhruv and his parents, seemingly oblivious to the whirlwind of thoughts that stormed through Aarya's mind, engaged in a discussion about samosas. Yes, samosas—the deep-fried pockets of deliciousness that had become an unexpected focal point of the conversation. Aarya's mom, ever the gracious host, boasted about her culinary skills and promised to serve the best samosas after they were done with the formalities.

Lost in her contemplation, Aarya found herself wondering if this was how it was meant to be—a complex dance between societal expectations and personal desires. Dhruv, a seemingly ideal match on paper, checked all the boxes: good looks, a stable job, and an apparent affection for Aarya. Yet, the situation felt surreal, like a scene from a movie where the protagonist is caught in a script not of her own making.

In the midst of her introspection, Aarya's attention snapped back to reality as Dhruv's mom directed a pointed question at her. "When are you finding an actual job, beta?" The question hung in the air, carrying with it an undercurrent of judgment and expectation. Aarya, momentarily caught off guard, rallied her thoughts, navigating the delicate balance between truth and the expectations of her potential in-laws.

The room, filled with the aroma of samosas and the weight of unspoken concerns, became a battleground where Aarya grappled with her own identity and the societal roles assigned to her. She couldn't shake the feeling that she was being assessed not for who she was, but for who she could potentially become in the eyes of her future in-laws. The samosas, delicious as they may be, couldn't mask the bitter taste of uncertainty that lingered in the air. The room echoed with the clash of societal norms and personal identity, leaving Aarya at the intersection of tradition and self-discovery.

Aarya's mom, sensing the brewing tension in the air, gave her a gentle nudge, a silent plea to respond politely to Dhruv's mom's inquiry. The unspoken message conveyed a mix of maternal concern and the weight of societal expectations, leaving Aarya torn between her own convictions and the desire to adhere to the norms laid out for her.

Dad, ever the diplomat, picked up on the palpable discomfort and swiftly intervened. He smoothly shifted the conversation to a more neutral territory—the potential wedding venue. Attempting to diffuse the tension, he sprinkled the discussion with a few of his trademark dad jokes, hoping to steer the gathering back to lighter, less contentious ground.

Amidst the forced laughter prompted by dad's jokes, Aarya couldn't shake off the feeling of disappointment. It wasn't directed at the probing question or Dhruv's mom; instead, it lingered in the unspoken silence of her parents. She expected her mom, her staunch supporter, to speak up, to assert her daughter's choices. Instead, the silence spoke volumes, leaving Aarya feeling abandoned.

What about Dhruv? Aarya stole glances at Dhruv, wondering if he shared the same turmoil she was experiencing. Why hadn't he spoken up when his mom asked about her job? Did he feel the same way about her job or did he also feel trapped in the expectations set by his family, just as she did? The silence between them became a chasm, and Aarya couldn't fathom why Dhruv hadn't offered a word of reassurance or solidarity. It left her grappling with a sense of isolation, questioning the foundation of their connection. Was their understanding merely a facade, shattered under the weight of societal norms?

As the discussion about wedding venues unfolded, Aarya's mind raced with questions. Was she merely being prepped to fit into a predetermined role as someone's daughter-in-law? Why did her mother withhold her usual vocal support? The imbalance of attention and validation gnawed at her, sowing the seeds of betrayal. She yearned for the charade to end, eager to retreat from the spotlight that seemed to cast her in a role she hadn't auditioned for.

BRIDAL CHRONICLES: THEATRICS OF TRADITION - 1

In the picturesque town of Traditionsville, where societal norms ran amok, the "Khaandaan" family found themselves at the center of an intriguing saga – the impending wedding of their beloved daughter, "Beti". Little did they know that the wedding preparations would unveil a surreal transformation, turning their once-typical behaviour into a carnival of confusion, comedy, and unbridled theatrics.

Act 1: The Engagement Extravaganza

The tale began with the announcement of Beti's engagement to the charming "Daamaad". The Khaandaan family, once known for their pragmatic approach to life, was now swept away by the wave of matrimonial madness. Beti's father, Mr. Khaandaan, underwent a metamorphosis, trading his sensible demeanour for an air of wedding-induced hysteria.

The transformation was evident as Mr. Khaandaan dove headfirst into the world of wedding planning, consulting horoscopes, matchmaking experts, and even a mystic parrot rumoured to possess unparalleled matchmaking skills. The once-rational family discussions now revolved around auspicious wedding dates, elaborate guest lists, and the intricacies of matching wedding attire.

Act 2: The Dress Dilemmas

As the wedding attire became the focal point of familial debates, the family found themselves navigating the treacherous waters of fashion faux pas and colour conundrums. Mrs. Khaandaan, previously a champion of practicality, now became a connoisseur of bridal couture, attending fashion shows and scrutinizing bridal magazines with a fervour bordering on obsession.

In an attempt to please the ever-growing list of distant relatives, the family embarked on a quest for the perfect wedding ensemble. Mrs. Khaandaan, armed with a checklist that rivalled a military operation, marched through bridal boutiques like a general on a mission. The once-modest budget was discarded in favour of an extravagant ensemble that would make even the wealthiest of royalty blush.

Act 3: The Invitation Insanity

The battle of the invitations unfolded as the family found themselves entangled in a web of etiquette, social hierarchies, and familial egos. What was once a straightforward process became an exercise in diplomacy, as Mrs. Khaandaan negotiated the delicate balance of inviting distant relatives, long-lost acquaintances, and neighbours who may or may not have once complimented Beti on her impeccable taste in curtains.

The invitation list, initially a modest compilation of close friends and family, now resembled a phonebook. Mrs. Khaandaan, fuelled by a newfound zest for social standing, insisted on inviting everyone from the local grocer to the neighbourhood stray cat. The once-hospitable Khaandaan residence became a battlefield of social expectations, with each invitation carrying the weight of familial reputation.

Act 4: The Ritual Riddles

The arrival of the wedding rituals marked the peak of the family's transformation. The once-mundane household now resembled a film set, complete with costume changes, prop arrangements, and a director (Mr. Khaandaan) orchestrating every scene with unwavering authority.

Rituals, once solemn expressions of cultural heritage, now took on a surreal quality. Mr. Khaandaan, armed with a checklist that resembled a screenplay, directed the family through each tradition with military precision. The significance of each ritual was overshadowed by the meticulous choreography, leaving the family members wondering if they were participating in a wedding or a Broadway production.

Act 5: The Bridezilla Epidemic

Beti, the unwitting protagonist of this matrimonial drama, found herself caught in the crossfire of familial expectations. The once-relaxed bride-to-be was now dubbed "Bridezilla" by her own family, as the whirlwind of wedding preparations and the avalanche of advice from distant aunts and long-lost cousins transformed her into an unwitting diva.

The Khaandaan household, once a haven of familial harmony, now resembled a chaotic circus tent. Beti's once-ordinary requests became monumental tasks, subject to scrutiny and judgment from a panel of self-appointed wedding experts within the family. The simple act of choosing wedding favours morphed into a diplomatic negotiation, with family members staking claim to their preferred choices.

Act 6: The Grand Finale – The Wedding Day

As the wedding day dawned, the Khaandaan family found themselves in the throes of an emotional rollercoaster. Mrs. Khaandaan, having weathered the storm of wedding preparations, was a mix of nerves and excitement. The once-pragmatic family was now a congregation of emotional wrecks, all grappling with the surreal transformation that had overtaken their once-ordinary lives.

The wedding ceremony, initially intended as a celebration of love, became a grand spectacle of familial expectations. Mrs. Khaandaan, donned in her finest saree and armed with a checklist that had survived countless battles, marched Beti through the intricacies of the pheras, the rituals, and the inevitable family photoshoots that seemed to stretch into eternity.

CHAPTER 8

BRIDAL CHRONICLES: THEATRICS OF TRADITION - 2

Amidst the matrimonial mayhem, Beti began reminiscing her life. It seemed that from the moment she took her first steps into adolescence, the world had conspired to center every facet of her life around the impending grand event – her wedding.

The Sartorial Satire

From the very moment Beti traded her dolls for diaries, the narrative of her life secmed to be stitched into the fabric of bridal couture. As she ventured into the world of fashion, every sartorial choice became a prelude to the grand wedding ensemble. The closet, once a realm of personal expression, morphed into a runway of potential bridal/newly-wed looks. Every outfit was scrutinized not for its comfort or style but for its hypothetical compatibility with the elusive wedding lehenga that loomed on the horizon.

The Personality Pantomime

As Beti's personality blossomed like a comedic play, it found itself unwittingly entangled in the matrimonial script. Quirks that once defined her uniqueness became potential obstacles in the pursuit of the perfect daughter-in-law persona. Mrs. Khaandaan, armed with a checklist of desirable traits, nudged Beti towards the refined art of demure laughter and agreeable nods. The once-vibrant personality had to undergo an audition for societal approval, leaving behind a caricature of politeness that would make even the most seasoned actors blush.

The Career Carousel

Beti's journey through career choices felt like a carousel of societal expectations. Every profession she considered was judged not for its intrinsic value or her passion but for its perceived compatibility with the grand narrative of a married life. Mr. Khaandaan, now a self-proclaimed career counsellor, scrutinized each career option through the lens of marital bliss. The once-bold dreams were trimmed and tailored to fit the mould of a career that wouldn't overshadow the impending role of a dutiful wife.

The Subtle Suppression Symphony

In the symphony of Beti's life, a subtle suppression played as an underlying theme. Every opinion, every choice, and every ambition was subjected to the silent orchestration of societal norms. Mr and Mrs. Khaandaan, the unwitting conductors, ensured that Beti's individuality harmonized with the expectations of a bride-to-be. The cacophony of societal whispers drowned out the once-clear melody of Beti's aspirations, leaving behind a muted tune that echoed the matrimonial script.

As the echoes of matrimonial madness subsided, Beti found herself standing at the crossroads of tradition and her own aspirations. Unable to ignore the theatrical absurdity that had consumed her life, and in a moment of courageous clarity, she expressed her determination to break free from the suffocating mould of societal expectations. "Mom," she began, her voice steady but resolute, "I refuse to let my daughter endure the same farce that has defined my journey. Our lives should not be scripted by outdated norms, and I won't perpetuate this cycle of societal expectations."

Mrs. Khaandaan, momentarily taken aback by the assertiveness of her daughter, softened her gaze and sighed. "Beti," she responded, a hint of nostalgia in her eyes, "I once stood where you stand now. I vowed to break free from the chains of tradition and forge a different path. My mother said the same thing to her mother, and I, in turn, said it to mine. Yet, here we are, still entangled in the threads of societal expectations. It's a cycle that seems unbreakable, a tapestry woven through generations. Change comes slow, my dear, and often, the very roots we aim to sever are the ones that hold us in place."

In this poignant exchange, Beti glimpsed the weight of generational expectations that Mrs. Khaandaan had carried. The realization that societal norms had perpetuated through the ages, despite the best intentions, left both women standing on the precipice of tradition, questioning the threads that bound them and contemplating the possibility of rewriting their shared narrative.

* * *

Data Sparks and Sizzling Stats

As the highly anticipated podcast day dawned, Aarya found herself swaying on the edge of nervous anticipation. No matter how diligently she tried to contain her anxiety, it manifested in tiny beads of sweat that betrayed her inner turmoil. The deodorant, despite multiple reapplications, seemed like a futile attempt to quell the nervous energy that permeated her.

Pratik, ever the supportive colleague, attempted to soothe her frayed nerves with words of encouragement. Meera and Gouhrravv, faithful friends, stood by her side in the studio, offering moral support. However, their collective efforts seemed to only marginally alleviate the palpable tension in the air.

Then entered Kabir Singhania, the much-anticipated guest for the podcast. Far from the stereotypical image of a suited businessman, Kabir radiated a casual charm in his blue jeans and a simple black t-shirt. His tousled hair and easy-going attire belied the gravity of his success, portraying him as a man comfortable in his own skin. His expressive eyes twinkled with a mixture of wisdom and a light-hearted spirit that instantly put those around him at ease.

With an infectious smile, Kabir exuded an approachability that transcended the typical corporate persona. His hands, adorned with minimalistic accessories, gestured with purpose as he engaged in conversation. There was an effortless grace to his movements, and the warmth in his voice carried a genuine interest in the stories waiting to unfold. As he navigated the room, Kabir's unassuming presence became a powerful force, subtly commanding attention.

As Kabir suggested ordering coffee to foster a more relaxed environment, he surveyed the team for their preferences. Amidst the exchange, his perceptive gaze fell upon one individual whose reaction stood out—Aarya. In a moment frozen in time, she hadn't uttered a word but her open-mouthed astonishment spoke volumes.

Meera, sensing the potential embarrassment, swiftly intervened, nudging Aarya and rescuing her from the spotlight. Aarya, grateful for Meera's support, quickly collected herself, ready to engage in the upcoming podcast recording. Meanwhile, Meera, in her characteristic playful manner, subtly mocked Aarya, suggesting to Kabir, "You might want to get Aarya something decaf. It seems like she's had quite the caffeine boost today."

With the tension diffused and a light-hearted banter settling in, Aarya and Kabir seamlessly transitioned into the podcast. The recording flowed smoothly, showcasing the collective brilliance of the team. As they wrapped up, a sense of accomplishment and satisfaction filled the room.

Pratik was ecstatic. Kabir, impressed by the dynamic collaboration, extended a dinner invitation to Aarya.

The unexpected invitation left Aarya contemplating its nature—was it a casual post-podcast celebration, or did it carry the undertones of a potential date? The question lingered in the air, adding a layer of intrigue to an already eventful day.

* * *

Aarya, still deciphering the nature of Kabir's dinner invitation, accepted the offer and decided to play it safe. The quest for the perfect outfit, however, turned into a comedic ordeal. Raiding her closet like a detective on a mission, Aarya cycled through a zillion changes, each outfit dismissed for being either too formal or too casual, leaving her in a wardrobe-induced frenzy.

After much deliberation, she settled on what seemed like the most viable option—a pair of blue jeans paired with a simple black t-shirt. It was a classic choice, or so she thought. Little did she know that Kabir's evening attire had a different agenda. As she arrived at the restaurant, the sight before her eyes left her contemplating a swift escape to change. Kabir, contrary to his casual appearance that morning, was now adorned in a dapper suit, looking like he had just walked off the cover of a fashion magazine.

Caught off guard, Aarya scanned the surroundings, silently pondering if it was too late for a costume change. But before she could execute her retreat plan, Kabir spotted her and called out, "Aarya!" Trying to mask her wardrobe woes, she mustered a weary grin. To her surprise, Kabir complimented her attire with a sincere, "I love what you're wearing." Aarya couldn't help but question whether he was being polite or subtly sarcastic.

As they settled in for dinner, the ambiguity surrounding the dinner invitation began to unravel. Kabir, in a moment of candid honesty, thanked Aarya for accepting his invitation to a date. Aarya's internal monologue screamed, "What?" as she navigated the unexpected revelation, adding a touch of humour to the unfolding romantic comedy.

Aarya, dumbfounded by the sudden realization that her evening with Kabir had morphed into a date, found herself choking on her food in sheer surprise. In a swift and caring gesture, Kabir handed her a glass of water, concern etched on his face. "Are you okay?" he inquired, before playfully apologizing for not being clearer earlier. Aarya, still recovering from the unexpected twist, managed an awkward smile. The internal turmoil began as she wondered whether she should disclose her engagement to Kabir. The uncharted territory of dating felt like a maze, and she struggled to navigate the moral dilemmas.

As the evening unfolded, Aarya found herself captivated by Kabir's charm. The conversation flowed seamlessly, and for the first time, she let her guard down, genuinely enjoying the moment. Hours passed like minutes, and as the night neared its end, Kabir offered to drop her home. Pulling up to her apartment, the air thickened with anticipation. Just as Aarya prepared to exit the car, Kabir broke the silence with a quick remark, "I had a great time today," and leaned in toward her.

Aarya's heart raced as a myriad of thoughts flooded her mind. Was this it? Was the spell being broken? Was she about to experience her first kiss? The cinematic scenes of romantic encounters played in her mind, and she frantically tried to remember the details. Any practise she had was only on the back of her hand, after watching her first Korean TV series, back when she was in College. "God! The Unrealistic expectations those damn shows set", she thought. Wait, did she have onion or garlic for dinner? Did she need a breath mint? There's only one first kiss, after all. The pressure mounted, and Aarya felt like her brain was on the verge of explosion. As she contemplated an easier way out, Kabir leaned in and planted a gentle peck on her cheek. Whispering in her ear, he teased, "Next time!" Aarya flushed red, feeling a mix of embarrassment and excitement. With a soft "goodnight," she hastily made her exit, escaping into the safety of her apartment, her mind and heart still racing from the unexpected turn of events.

CHAPTER 10

LOVE BUG CHRONICLES

"Navigating Between Past Commitments and New Connections"

Aarya's morning kicked off with a lively video call with Meera, who was brimming with excitement. "Spill it, Aarya!" Meera exclaimed, her enthusiasm evident. "What happened? You're smiling like a smitten maniac," she teased, eager for all the juicy details. Aarya, still riding the wave of last night's emotions, recounted every little moment with Kabir, her face lighting up as she relived those cherished memories.

"Love bug, Aarya! You've been bitten!" Meera playfully declared, convinced that Aarya had fallen for Kabir. Aarya, however, hesitated. She was undeniably attracted to Kabir, not just physically but also by the captivating and effortless conversations they shared. It was a unique and unexplored feeling for her, different from anything she had experienced before.

As the girls dreamily played out the romantic scenarios in each other's heads, reality swiftly intruded when Aarya's phone buzzed. It was Dhruv! The girls snapped back to the present, reminded of the engagement that Aarya was already committed to. Aarya knew she couldn't avoid

Dhruv's messages indefinitely. Promising to update Meera soon, she reluctantly shifted her attention to Dhruv.

* * *

Aarya's phone buzzed persistently with Dhruv's concerned inquiries. "Where have you been, Aarya? I've been trying to reach you all week! Is everything alright? Are you alright?" His words were a cascade of questions, filled with genuine concern. Aarya, guilt washing over her, finally picked up and greeted him with a hesitant, "Hi Dhruv! Sorry about that." She felt a pang of remorse for unintentionally shutting him out and realized she had been ignorant of his feelings.

In an attempt to bridge the gap, Aarya eagerly shared her recent professional developments. "I was busy at work. You see, we are exploring new opportunities that could provide an excellent platform for my channel." Her excitement about work spilled into her words as she hoped to convey the positive aspects of her life.

"Yeah, yeah, Aarya, I know you are doing great at work, I know you are busy. We all are! But you have to take care of yourself, you know. And our wedding is just a month away. There is so much to do before that," Dhruv interjected, abruptly shifting the conversation. Aarya was taken aback, her enthusiasm for work overshadowed by the unexpected revelation. "Wait, what wedding?" she asked, disbelief colouring her voice.

Dhruv, with a hint of jest, dropped the bombshell, "Our wedding, of course, silly!" Aarya's heart skipped a beat. The weight of his words settled into her reality, leaving her stunned. Before she could gather her thoughts, Dhruv's jovial tone lingered in the air. "Umm, Dhruv, let me call you back," Aarya stammered, hanging up abruptly. The room seemed to close in around her as she grappled with the sudden twist in her life's narrative.

Aarya's frantic voice pierced through the phone as she screamed, "What wedding, Ma?" Her mother, seemingly unaware of the chaos that had unfolded, responded with a cheerful tone, "Your wedding, beta! We have been trying to reach you all week. Your dad and I are so stressed. There is so little time and so much to do."

The shock reverberated in Aarya's voice as she struggled to comprehend the sudden turn of events. "When, how did this all happen so fast?" she interrupted, her mind a whirlwind of confusion. Aarya's mother, seemingly unfazed, began to explain, "Arey! Remember the Babaji that Latha aunty used to go to? Dhruv's family are his devotees, and they approached him, requesting him to set a date for the wedding. It apparently is a very auspicious day. You are so lucky!"

Aarya's emotions, already on edge, boiled over. "Well, who was gonna ask me?" she fumed, tears streaming down her face now. Her mother, still oblivious to Aarya's distress, continued, "Ask what? What happened, Aarya?

Are you feeling okay? You are engaged to be married. You have chosen your partner yourself, and we gladly accepted your decision. You are 28 already. I had you when I was 21. There is a time for these things, beta! You can't just keep delaying these things, Aarya. Your father and I are so worried for you. Don't spoil your life." Unable to bear the weight of her mother's words, Aarya hung up, the gravity of the situation sinking in.

Aarya paced back and forth in her apartment, her mind racing with a myriad of emotions and the words "Our wedding, of course, Silly!" echoing in her mind. How did this happen? Why was Dhruv planning a wedding without even discussing it with her? Why did her parents not ask her anything? The excitement she had felt just moments ago about her work accomplishments, and of course, her date with Kabir was replaced by an overwhelming sense of confusion.

Feeling a surge of frustration, Aarya dialled Meera's number again. This time, her voice carried a tone of urgency and anxiety. "Meera, you won't believe what Dhruv just told me. He mentioned our wedding is in a month, and I had no idea about it," Aarya confessed, her words stumbling over each other.

Meera, on the other end of the line, gasped in surprise. "What? A wedding? Is this some kind of prank?" Meera questioned, her mind trying to process the unexpected turn of events. Aarya explained the bizarre conversation with Dhruv, and the call with her mom afterward, and Meera advised her to call Dhruv back for clarification as things seemed to have gotten out of hand.

Reluctantly, Aarya took a deep breath and dialled Dhruv's number once again. As the call connected, she braced herself for the impending conversation, uncertain about the answers she would receive.

"Dhruv! We need to talk."

UNVEILING ECHOES

The ambiance of the upscale restaurant, typically a haven for laughter, whispered conversations, and the clinking of glasses, now morphed into an unfamiliar tension as Dhruv and Aarya found themselves seated across each other in the exclusive privacy of the dining area he had thoughtfully reserved. Dhruv, a usually stoic figure radiating calmness and playfulness, failed to conceal the palpable anxiety that lingered in his eyes. Aarya, adorned in an attire carefully chosen for this moment, had meticulously rehearsed the impending conversation in her mind countless times. She understood the profound importance of honesty, especially when navigating the intricate landscape of matters of the heart.

In this cocoon of apprehension, Aarya took a deep breath, bravely shattering the silence that seemed to tighten its grip on the space between them. "Dhruv, we need to talk," she began, her voice steady yet carrying an underlying solemnity that sent ripples through the charged air. Dhruv, now visibly concerned, leaned in, a mixture of eagerness and trepidation etched across his face, eager to grasp the nature of the conversation that loomed ominously over them.

As Aarya uttered the weighty words, "I think we should call it off, Dhruv," a palpable wave of horror washed over him. Speechless and unable to conceal his distress any longer, Dhruv stammered, "What do you mean, Aarya? What went wrong? How could you say something like that at all?" His eyes, wide with shock, pleaded for an explanation, searching Aarya's face for any signs of uncertainty.

"I'm sorry, Dhruv. I know I should have said something sooner," Aarya began, her gaze remaining steady yet saturated with apologetic sincerity. "It all just happened so fast! We got engaged on our second date, and we never discussed a wedding! I have given this a lot of thought, and I think it would be better if we broke it off now than later."

Dhruv, caught off guard and grappling with the sudden unravelling of their relationship, attempted to fathom the gravity of Aarya's decision. The intimate ambiance, once a vessel for shared laughter and romantic conversations, now bore witness to an unexpected dissolution of ties. The conversation unfolded in a back-and-forth that seemed to echo the tumultuous emotions swirling around them, leaving Aarya with a heavy heart as she handed back the engagement ring.

The air grew denser with unspoken words and unfulfilled dreams. Aarya, feeling the weight of the situation, offered another apology, paid her share of the bill, and quietly departed from the restaurant. The chapter that had started with joyous celebrations and dreams of a shared future now concluded with the painful acknowledgment that some ties were not destined to endure.

In the wake of this emotional tempest, Aarya found herself ruminating on the events leading up to this momentous meeting. The day prior, she had grappled with the decision of whether to disclose her recent encounter with Kabir to Dhruv. However, a profound realization dawned upon her - her engagement with Dhruv wasn't solely influenced by her interaction with Kabir. The uncertainty had already taken root even before Kabir entered the picture. The previous night, when Kabir had extended another invitation for a date, she had disclosed her engagement, emphasizing the need for time to navigate through her emotions. Kabir, understanding her predicament, had gracefully accepted the situation and encouraged her to reach out whenever she felt ready.

As Aarya distanced herself from the restaurant, she knew she needed to focus on making things right for herself. The complexities of her emotions and the intricacies of her life demanded attention. The path ahead was uncertain, but she was resolute in her commitment to navigate it with integrity and clarity, determined to sculpt a future that resonated with authenticity and personal fulfilment.

CHAPTER 12

THE FINAL CHAPTER

The day dawned with a soft glow, the sun breaking through the dissipating clouds after a night of relentless rain. The air was crisp, carrying the scent of wet earth and the promise of new beginnings. Aarya, adorned in a simple yet elegant saree, stood before the mirror, a cascade of flowers gracefully weaving through her bun. Her reflection betrayed a mix of emotions—anticipation, nostalgia, and a subtle radiance that hinted at the transformation within.

As Aarya stepped into the awaiting cab, the world outside seemed to mirror her emotional landscape. The weather, once tempestuous, had now settled into a serene calm. Sunbeams played hide-and-seek through the parting clouds, casting a warm glow on the city streets. Aarya's cab wound its way through a landscape adorned with rain-kissed foliage, a tableau of nature mirroring the renewal unfolding within her.

In the quiet confines of the cab, Aarya allowed her mind to wander through the tapestry of the past few months. The decision to call off the wedding, though tumultuous, had paved the way for introspection and newfound purpose. She felt a tinge of guilt for not being present during the significant moments in her friends' lives. Meera and Gouhrravv's love had deepened, while Kriya and Shipra had taken a decisive step toward shared futures by moving in together.

Pratik, once an assistant and now Aarya's manager, had injected vitality into the podcast, transforming it into a vibrant success. The journey had been one of self-discovery and rekindling connections, an odyssey that prepared her for the profound moment awaiting her at the registrar's office.

The cab pulled up, and Aarya, with a heart brimming with emotions, stepped into the embrace of friends who awaited her at the registrar's office. Gouhrravv, ever the theatrical soul, greeted her with enthusiasm, acknowledging the transformative glow that enveloped her. Meera's warm hug conveyed unspoken camaraderie, and as a group, they entered the registrar's room, where promises would be sealed.

Kabir, a silent architect of Aarya's recent joys, entered behind them, offering a sincere apology for his slight delay. His presence added a layer of anticipation to the room, and the traditional kurta he adorned marked a departure from the Kabir they had known before.

The registrar's room, a canvas for unions, was filled with a palpable energy. Laughter and joy reverberated off the walls, creating an atmosphere where bonds were not just acknowledged but celebrated. Aarya, still basking in the camaraderie of her friends, stepped forward to sign the registrar's directory with Kabir.

And just like that, Meera and Gouhrravv were now married! Resounding cheers and heartfelt congratulations filled the room, echoing the collective celebration of a union that signified the end of a journey marked by unexpected twists, turns, and the anticipation of a radiant future. Aarya, casting her gaze around at her friends, couldn't suppress the overwhelming sense of gratitude for the delicate threads of fate that intricately wove together this singular and joyous mosaic of life.

www.ingramcontent.com/pod-product-compliance
Lightning Source LLC
Chambersburg PA
CBHW021405150726
47989CB00005B/2411